Something splashed in the darkness

The sentry peered cautiously down at the river from the pier's edge. He thought he could make out a vague shadow near the solid blackness of the pillars, and he slid the M-70 from his shoulder.

He had just pulled his flashlight from his pocket and turned it on when a voice called out in a harsh whisper. "Hey." Surprised, he swiveled in the direction of the sound, pulling a weak wash of light with him. He was confronted by a faint glimmer that was reflected from the lens of a diver's mask. The sentry's frozen mind wanted to send a command to his trigger finger, but he was distracted by a strange kind of swift and silent movement, like the winging of a bat.

A long, slender projectile streaked upward and plunged under his chin, penetrating the base of his skull. As he started to fall, his dying sight filled with a final image of a black figure rising from the water and looking on with grim satisfaction.

Mack Bolan's
PHOENIX FORCE.

PHOENIX FORCE.

GAR WILSON

BELGRADE DECEPTION

A GOLD EAGLE BOOK FROM

WORLDWIDE.

TORONTO · NEW YORK · LONDON · PARIS
AMSTERDAM · STOCKHOLM · HAMBURG
ATHENS · MILAN · TOKYO · SYDNEY

First edition July 1988

ISBN 0-373-61336-9

Special thanks and acknowledgment to
William Fieldhouse for his contribution to this work.

1

The crack of high-velocity bullets breaking the sound barrier echoed through the streets of Belgrade. A young actress who had just emerged from the Yugoslav Drama Theater along Marsala Tita Boulevard was the first victim. She was walking toward the street when a 7.62 mm bullet slammed into her forehead. Her pretty face awash in fresh blood, her long black hair smeared with brain tissue and skull fragments, she tumbled to the sidewalk.

The actress's companions cried out and ran for cover as the sniper chose a second target. A bearded old man hobbling up the steps of the main post office heard the shot that claimed the life of the actress. He turned toward the sound and a bullet ripped into his throat. The projectile blasted apart vertebrae at the nape of his neck and tore out an exit wound as big as a half dollar. The man's body sprawled down the steps as more shots erupted from a location along Kneza Milosa.

The sniper then began shooting at passing vehicles. The driver of a bus traveling along Kneza Milosa suddenly collapsed across the steering wheel when two 7.62 mm messengers of death punched through his windshield and shattered his face. The bus went out of control and swerved into the back of a beer truck. Passengers shrieked as they were violently tossed about inside the bus upon impact.

The truck was forced over the curb. The driver fought the wheel, but he could not steer the rig around the horrified pair of pedestrians who had been strolling along the sidewalk. The driver cried out in grief and astonishment as his vehicle hit the two middle-aged women laden with bags of groceries. Bread, vegetables and canned goods rolled into the gutter as the women were crushed under the wheels.

The next victim was a factory worker driving himself and two companions home from work. He had tried to avoid Kneza Milosa because he'd noticed some sort of disturbance. He had heard something that sounded like gunshots, but his co-workers had assured him the sounds were only backfires from some passing vehicle.

A bullet through the window on the driver's side proved how wrong that theory was. The driver's jawbone was smashed by the merciless copper-jacketed hornet. Shards of broken glass ripped into the flesh of the wounded driver and his unlucky passengers. The car swung out of control at the corner of Nemanjina and Sarajevska and crashed into the metal post of a street lamp. Metal crumpled amid a shower of shattered glass as the car folded up on impact. The stalk of the street lamp bent and the light bowed over the roof of the crippled car.

Thrown headfirst through the wrecked windshield, the driver no longer felt the pain of his bullet-smashed jaw as his throat was sliced open by jagged glass and consciousness mercifully left him. His companions survived the crash with only numerous cuts, broken bones and internal injuries. One man whose neck was severely sprained would spend several months wearing a brace. Neither of the survivors would be quite the same after the accident.

More shots shattered shop and restaurant windows along Kneza Milosa. Passersby rushed for cover and patrons inside the establishments ducked under furniture for shelter. A waiter in a Gypsy-style restaurant was not lucky enough to find cover in time. A bullet caught him between the shoulder blades and sent him screaming to the floor, his backbone split in two.

There were a lot of frightened shouts for help, but there was no evidence that any kind of assistance was on its way.

Long terrible minutes of terror passed before the wailing cry of police sirens announced that help had finally arrived. Uniformed policemen emerged from their vehicles parked along Kneza and Marsala Tita. Despite confusing reports, the police had managed to isolate the danger area. At last they were able to spot the sniper with binoculars. They had to keep their distance because the unknown rifleman was obviously armed with a long-range weapon and did not appear to be particular about whom he was shooting. There was no reason to believe he would hesitate to gun down a Belgrade police officer.

"There!" a patrolman declared, pointing a white-gloved finger at a large gray building surrounded by a tall iron gate. "That is the gunman's hiding place! I saw the barrel of his rifle at a second-story window."

The sergeant beside him nodded grimly in confirmation. "And I know what that building is. It's the American embassy."

"America?" the patrolman said, puzzled. "I know they are capitalists and opposed to our socialist way of life, but I didn't think Yugoslavia and America were truly enemies."

"I don't know what in hell is going on here," the police sergeant admitted. "All I know is that lunatic is killing Yugoslavian civilians. Women, old men, possibly children. I care who the son of a diseased sow might be. We can't let him get away with this."

"We're not going to storm the American embassy either, Sergeant," Police Captain Crnjanski announced as he approached the men. "That would be the same as attacking the United States of America."

"Appears to me the United States is attacking us, Captain," the sergeant replied glumly.

A tall athletic man in his early forties, Crnjanski simply grunted in a noncommittal manner. He removed his service cap and combed the fingers of one hand through the close-cropped sandy hair above his high forehead. This was not the sort of matter the police militia was qualified or authorized to handle, Crnjanski realized. Yet he, too, felt the anger and frustration expressed by the sergeant. What good police official would not feel the same way?

The captain held a pair of binoculars to his eyes as he leaned around the corner of a tailor shop across the street from the embassy. The leafy green branches of a tree beyond the iron gates of the embassy blocked his view of the window, but he was still able to glimpse the barrel of the sniper's rifle poking above the sill. Sunlight flashed on the lens of a telescopic sight mounted on the weapon.

"The delay between shots suggests the gunman is armed with a bolt-action or perhaps a semiautomatic rifle," Crnjanski remarked. "The bastard must be a trained marksman. He doesn't seem to have any trouble hitting targets four hundred meters away."

"What should we do, Captain?" the patrolman asked.

"Roadblocks are being set up to keep traffic out of this area," Crnjanski said, rubbing his lantern jaw with the palm of his hand. "I'm sure someone from the Federal Assembly is already in touch with the Americans."

"There must be something else we can do," the sergeant remarked.

"Lieutenant Zeleno is supervising the evacuation of civilians from the area," Crnjanski commented. "You men assist him, and please get the megaphone from my car. I'm going to try to talk to the Americans. Try to find out what's going on and perhaps get the sniper to surrender."

"I doubt if he will, sir."

"Perhaps not, but if nothing else it may get the bastard's attention for a while, during which he won't be shooting innocent people. It may also give the Americans inside the embassy time to overpower this maniac."

"Unless he's acting on their orders," the sergeant said with a suspicious glare at the embassy. "I say you can't trust any of those capitalists. Look what they did in Vietnam...."

"The Soviets are Communists and we certainly can't trust them," Crnjanski reminded the sergeant. "Look what they're *still* doing in Vietnam. To say nothing of Poland and Afghanistan. The Americans are not insane. I doubt they'd condone this sort of butchery. Some maniac must have simply gone berserk...."

Another shot erupted from the sniper's weapon. A bullet struck the flank of a car parked across from the embassy, and gasoline spilled from the ruptured fuel tank. A sudden burst of automatic fire startled the cops as the gunman sprayed the damaged vehicle with a salvo of bullets that sparked against metal and ignited the gasoline. The tank exploded, blasting the car to bits and spewing flaming debris across the cobblestone street.

The sergeant cursed as he recoiled from the edge of the tailor shop. "That wasn't a semiautomatic rifle!"

"No," Captain Crnjanski agreed grimly. "I'll need an English interpreter."

"What?" the patrolman asked, his ears still ringing from the explosion.

Crnjanski repeated the sentence, and a look of understanding dawned on the other man's face.

"I speak English, sir," the patrolman announced. "I studied it at the University of Novi Sad. Foreign language courses were encouraged because they claimed tourism would become an important source of income for the Yugoslav economy—"

"That's very nice," Crnjanski said brusquely, cutting the kid off. He realized the younger man was rambling because he was nervous about getting any closer to the psycho marksman. Crnjanski didn't blame the patrolman a bit. "Get the megaphone, please."

Taking the bullhorn from the captain's car, the patrolman joined Crnjanski as he ran to the side door of the tailor shop. Both policemen entered the building. The tailor and his customers had already been evacuated, so they had the place to themselves.

A clothing dummy surprised Crnjanski, and he clawed the holstered M-57 pistol on his hip before he realized the headless, armless humanoid torso on a metal stalk was not alive. Silly reaction, the captain thought. The enemy was across the street, lurking in the embassy or in an abandoned building nearby. Crnjanski figured tension had caused his reaction. He was glad a civilian hadn't been in the shop. The captain might have drawn his pistol and pointed it at the poor fellow.

There were several racks of suit jackets and trousers, piles of fabric on tables and pin cushions and tape measures and other tools of the tailor's trade all around. One of the windows had been shattered by a bullet. It was ironic to think that the tailor had probably been envied his shop locale because it was close to the American embassy, which meant he'd get lots of business from the American personnel. No doubt he wasn't so pleased with the location after the rifle round blasted through the window.

Crouching, Captain Crnjanski and the young patrolman headed for the windows. Crnjanski motioned the patrolman to get beside the gaping window, warning him not to stand up and become a target for the sniper. The captain handed the young officer the bullhorn and told him what to say.

"Attention! Attention!" the youth bellowed through the amplified megaphone. "This is the military police. We are ordering you to throw out your weapons and surrender at once. If you continue in this aggressive and criminal manner, we will be forced to respond with deadly retaliation. Police marksmen are already in position to..."

A salvo of automatic fire interrupted the patrolman. Bullets smashed the windowpane and sent glass shrapnel hurtling inside the shop. The young officer ducked, hugging the floor until the shooting ceased. He waited a full minute before raising his head. Bits of broken glass fell from his hair, and a ribbon of blood oozed from his scalp.

"I don't think this is going to work, Captain," he began as he glanced about the room. "Captain?"

Captain Crnjanski lay sprawled under another window, which had received a volley of high-velocity hailstones. The senior officer hadn't ducked in time. His eyes were open although a shard of glass had landed on the top lid of his right eye. A rifle slug had pierced the bridge of his nose and tunneled into his brain.

"Captain..." the patrolman whispered as he stared at the corpse. He trembled with fear, and his stomach turned with repulsion and terror. "What do I do now?"

2

"I bet you guys can guess why I called for this meeting," Hal Brognola began, chewing on the butt of an unlit cigar as if he wanted to bite through it. "The whole goddamn world is shocked by what happened in Belgrade, Yugoslavia yesterday."

The five men of Phoenix Force sat quietly at the conference table of the War Room in the Stony Man operations headquarters. Brognola was quite right. Each member of the special commando team had suspected why he'd been called in for a meeting. They also realized it probably meant the Fed was ready to assign them a new mission and the details would unfold as Brognola continued.

"As I'm sure you know," the top Fed in the nation said as he opened a folder in front of him on the table, "eight people were killed and more than a dozen injured by that sniper incident in Belgrade. Of course, the worst part of this disaster is the fact that the gunman was shooting at Yugoslavians from *inside* the American embassy there. The son of a bitch was actually shooting from the window of the ambassador's office.''

"According to the news report I heard on the radio, the ambassador was also murdered by the gunman before the assassin took his own life,'' Yakov Katzenelenbogen remarked. The middle-aged Israeli veteran of a thousand battlefields tapped a pack of Camels against the steel hooks of the prosthesis at the end of his right arm to loosen a cigarette from the container. "The assassin hasn't yet been identified, but he was not a member of the embassy staff and his nationality has yet to be confirmed.''

"The Yugoslavians are saying the evidence suggests Ambassador Woodland committed suicide with a pistol found next to his body when the Marines finally broke down the door to the office,'' the Fed explained. "The ambassador's brains were smeared all over the wall next to his desk. The assassin also appears to have given himself a bullet-lobotomy. It's true he wasn't one of the embassy personnel, but they did find identification on the corpse.''

"What kind of identification?'' Gary Manning inquired. A brawny Canadian with a near-genius IQ, Manning was a quiet, stoic man who didn't like making any sort of assumption until all available facts had been gathered. One of the best explosives and demolitions experts in the world, Manning was accustomed to working with materials that left no room for error.

He knew a mistake based on incorrect data could be fatal. "Passport? Driver's license? Credit cards?"

"Military dog tags for Franklin P. Cadder," Brognola answered, consulting a computer printout sheet on the table. "I had Aaron tap into the personnel records of the Defense Department and he discovered that a Cadder, Franklin P., served in Vietnam with the United States Army. He vanished in 1970 and has been listed as missing in action ever since. The social security number, blood type and religious preference on the dog tags are the same as those on record for Sergeant E-5 Franklin Cadder, who's been MIA for the past eighteen years."

"Do they know for sure the sniper in Belgrade is Cadder?" Calvin James asked. The tall black man from the south side of Chicago was a Vietnam veteran himself and didn't like the idea that a fellow American fighting man from the Southeast Asian conflict might turn out to be the mad sniper of Belgrade.

"Nobody can be sure of much of anything just yet, except that a lot of innocent people got killed and relations between the United States and Yugoslavia are going to be lower than whale shit—which sinks to the bottom of the ocean," Brognola stated, casting a troubled look at the others around the table. "America's image throughout the world is already suffering from this incident."

"I imagine it is," Rafael Encizo commented, his handsome dark features showing his concern. He had a good understanding of international relationships.

"Naturally, it's being compared to what happened at the Libyan embassy in London back in 1984," Brognola continued. "And that similar incident at the Mardarajan embassy, which I'm sure you guys remember. I know I'll never forget it."

"Bloody hell," David McCarter groaned. The foxfaced Briton was getting irritable waiting for the Fed to get around to telling them exactly what their next mission would be. A former sergeant in the British SAS, McCarter thrived on excitement and hated wasting precious time that he felt could be better spent rushing to where the action was. "You're not still bent out of shape about that Mardarajan business, are you, Hal?"

"The President chewed off enough of my ass that I still have trouble sitting down," the Fed answered. "He wasn't too happy when you guys hit that embassy in London. It was an unauthorized mission and it could have been an international scandal, since raiding that embassy was virtually an act of war on the country of Mardaraja."

"That was more than two years ago, Hal," Katz reminded Brognola. "There was no scandal, there was no war and the republic of Mardaraja doesn't exist any longer. What might have happened is really a moot point now."

"You five hot dogs were acting on your own and there were television cameras all over the place." Brognola sighed. "There'll be lots of televised coverage at Belgrade, too. You're gonna have to keep a low profile there. None of that grand-slam stuff you guys specialize in."

"Then what the hell are you sending us to Yugoslavia for?" McCarter asked crossly, taking a pack of Players cigarettes from the breast pocket of his wrinkled sport jacket and cockily returning Encizo's disapproving glare. Encizo was a militant nonsmoker, and just then his patience was in short supply. "Sounds like you need a bunch of bleedin' diplomats, not Phoenix Force."

"The President wants you guys on this mission," Brognola explained. "You know how the chain of command works for Stony Man. The man in the Oval Office tells me what he wants. I map out the mission and assign it to you and the other men with our outfit. Frankly, nobody knows what the hell is going on in Belgrade. We don't know if the sniper really was Cadder or an enemy agent."

"He could have been both," Encizo mused. The Cuban was a veteran of the Bay of Pigs invasion and he had spent time in one of Castro's political prisons. "If Cadder was captured by the Communists in Vietnam, it's possible he's been turned. Soviet advisors could have shipped him off to Moscow, and the KGB could have spent the past eighteen years brainwashing and conditioning him to carry out one suicide mission. Look what they did to Raul.''

Raul was Encizo's younger brother. He had been taken to a reeducation camp by the Communists and indoctrinated to accept the new order in Cuba. In fact, Rafael Encizo had recently discovered Raul was a paratrooper captain in Castro's army. Raul Encizo had become a highly dedicated officer in the Cuban military. More than that, Rafael's kid brother appeared to be a fanatic and a highly trained killing machine. When they had last met during a mission in Colombia, Raul had tried to kill his elder brother and damned near succeeded.

''Your brother was just a kid when the Communists went to work on educating him for their own purposes,'' Manning reminded Encizo, his voice soft and even. The Canadian warrior realized the knowledge that Raul was fighting for the other side was very hard on Rafael. ''What was he? Five at the time? Cadder was an adult and it would be considerably more difficult to turn him, unless the guy had already developed some pretty strong feelings against the United States before the KGB got their hands on him.''

''Difficult, but not impossible,'' Encizo insisted.

''Well, you fellas can try to find out when you get to Belgrade,'' Brognola declared. ''Make no mistake on this, gentlemen. This mission is goddamn important. There's a hell of a lot at stake here.''

"Definitely," Katz agreed with a nod. "Yugoslavia is a Communist country, with a one-party system, but it isn't in the Soviet camp. Yugoslavian socialism allows for a lot of corruption, just like in the Soviet Union, but despite the country's ties to the Kremlin, it is also on very good terms with the United States and other Western democracies. I'm sure Uncle Sam wants to keep it that way. If Yugoslavia decides the United States is its enemy, it might slide toward the Soviets and eventually wind up under control by Moscow."

"That's right," Brognola confirmed. "There's also the high probability that America will become less trusted and respected throughout the world because of this incident. Newspapers all over the world have printed stories about psychos in Texas who mount towers and open fire on crowds below. A nut in California starts shooting at people inside a fast food restaurant. These are some of the publicized images of life in America. If the folks abroad start worrying that there might be a deranged killer in our embassies, Yugoslavia won't be the only nation to sever diplomatic relations with us. This makes us look as if we're no better than Khaddafi's gunmen at the Libyan embassy in London."

"Yugoslavia plans to break relations with the U.S. now?" Manning asked.

"Not yet," Brognola answered. "But the president of Yugoslavia has been in touch with our President and it doesn't sound good. The Yugoslavians are willing to listen to our explanations of the incident, but so far we don't have any. That's why the President wants Phoenix Force to handle this. You guys get results."

"We're not diplomats or criminal investigators, Hal," Katz said, crushing his cigarette in an onyx ashtray. "David is right about that."

"You won't be working with diplomats," the Fed assured them. "We've already arranged for your connections with the Yugoslavian Federal Security Committee. You'll be working with them. Necessary clearance and identification papers are being taken care of. Cover names will be ones you've used in the past. You'll be able to transport weapons and other equipment without problems with customs...."

"Sounds wonderful," Manning said without enthusiasm. "But what are we supposed to do that the Yugoslavian authorities can't do just as well or better?"

"One reason you're going is to show the Yugoslavians we're trying to do everything possible to clear up this mess," Brognola answered.

"I knew it," McCarter complained. The Briton had become too restless to remain seated. He'd started to pace around the conference table. "Bleedin' politics again! They want us to go to Yugoslavia so it'll make a good impression, even though this sort of thing isn't our bloody job. We work search-and-destroy missions. Terrorists, enemy agents running a nasty conspiracy, criminal syndicates—those are the kind of targets we go after...."

"Yeah," Brognola said with a sigh. "I'm familiar with what Phoenix Force does, David. I was here when Mack Bolan first put you guys together and I've been chief of operations at Stony Man ever since. If I look kind of familiar to you, that's the reason."

"Davie has a point," Calvin James said with a shrug. "After all, you're shipping us off to a Communist country, Hal, even if it is on fairly good terms with the Western nations. There's a real good chance the KGB will be active there. Hell, they might be responsible for the shooting. You mentioned the press already. That's another big problem."

"Nobody's mentioned what could be the worst situation for Phoenix Force," Encizo began. "If the Federal Assembly decides to sever relations with the U.S. while we're in Yugoslavia, we might wind up being arrested as enemy agents and either traded back to the West—as long as we're discussing potential nightmares—even handed over to the Soviets if Yugoslavia decides to strengthen ties with them. If the KGB even vaguely suspects who we are, we'd be in one hell of a bad situation."

"We'd be lucky if they just had us shot," McCarter muttered.

"If you guys want to refuse this mission..." Brognola began, although he had never imagined this would happen.

"That's not why we're going on about what might go wrong," Katz stated, confidently speaking for all members of Phoenix Force. Having worked with them for several years, he knew them as well as he knew himself. "We've all faced high risks before and that doesn't worry us, but it *does* bother us to think we're being sent on a mission that we're not really qualified for. Risking your life is one thing, but taking on high risk when the odds of success are practically none is quite a different matter."

"Okay," Brognola said with a solemn nod. "Let me explain something. If it turns out the gunman was Cadder and he went crazy somehow, we want you to help cover up as much of the embarrassing facts as possible. If that means you have to steal evidence and destroy it or manufacture new evidence, you do it."

"Jesus," Calvin James said with disgust. "I don't like this sort of crap, Hal."

"Like it or not," the Fed insisted, "we want to keep Uncle Sam's skirts as clean as possible. The President doesn't need another scandal and this country doesn't need to lose face to the rest of the world. We can't afford it."

"Okay," Gary Manning replied, apparently accepting this explanation as logical enough. "What if it turns out the KGB or somebody else is really responsible for the Belgrade incident?"

"Then you make damn sure they don't get away with it," Brognola declared firmly. "That's the main reason the President wants Phoenix Force to handle this. He thinks this is some sort of enemy action, a plot to discredit the United States and all it stands for. If it's true, he wants you to make sure the enemy pays for this stunt. You guys have a great track record for this sort of work. Nobody gets away from Phoenix Force.''

3

Phoenix Force received its first view of Yugoslavia from 20,000 feet through the windows of the JAT (Yugoslavian Airlines) jet. The largest of the Balkan peninsula countries of southeastern Europe, Yugoslavia seemed very green and peaceful from the sky. Much of Yugoslavia consists of hills and mountains and almost a third of the country is still forested.

As the plane approached Belgrade, the passengers saw the capital city from the air. Although Yugoslavia was not united as a country until 1918, the city of Belgrade has existed since the third century B.C. when it was known as Singidinum. Located in the very heart of the Balkans, it has been seized and occupied by many invading forces throughout history, including the Romans, Celts, Huns, Goths, Byzantines, Bulgars, Hungarians and Turks. Austrian troops held the city in World War I, German forces during World War II.

Belgrade reflects a pleasant combination of old-world charm and modern progress. This is evident in the mixed architecture of buildings, old and new, within the city. Byzantine, Moorish and Ottoman structures stand alongside modern office buildings and high rises.

The JAT airliner descended to a runway of the international airport not far from Tasmajdan Park. Phoenix Force deplaned with the other passengers, mostly Italians and a few other Western Europeans. Since the sniper incident in Belgrade, all flights to Yugoslavia from the United States had been suspended and no JAT planes were permitted to travel to America. Phoenix Force had had to travel to an American military base in Italy and get a JAT flight out of Rome to Belgrade.

Two men waited for them at customs. A tall, physically fit figure clad in an unseasonal dark gray suit stood with his arms folded on his well-developed chest. His companion was a short, toadlike man with wide, thin lips and bulging eyes, further exaggerated by glasses with lenses as thick as the bottoms of twin beer mugs. The Phoenix group recognized Lieutenant Colonel Ivo Mazuranic and Major Petar Selimovic from descriptions Brognola had given them at Stony Man headquarters. The Yugoslavian security agents had probably received a general description of the five visitors as well, but the pair barely glanced at Phoenix Force as the five men approached.

"Bonjour, monsieur," Yakov Katzenelenbogen began, using the password in French that Stony Man and the Yugoslav authorities had decided upon for

security. *"Pouvez-vous prendre mes bagages, s'il vous plaît?"*

"Ich verstehe nicht," the shorter Yugoslav answered in German with an apologetic shrug. *"Sprechen Sie Deutsche?"*

"Ja," Katz said with a nod. "How about English?"

"We speak some of that, too," the taller Yugoslav said dryly with a curt nod. "We'll waive customs to get your luggage through. By the way, your French accent is quite convincing."

"Thank you," Katz said modestly. He did not tell the agent he had actually been born in France. Yakov's father had been a master linguist originally from Russia. Katz spoke six languages fluently, with proper regional accents, and had an adequate command of several other languages. Unfortunately, Serbo-Croatian—the most common language in Yugoslavia—was not one he had mastered. "This is a rather awkward way to make introductions."

"Social pleasantries will have to wait," the tall Yugoslav declared in a firm, less-than-friendly tone. "Please follow us, gentlemen."

Formal introductions were not exchanged until they left the airport terminal in a limousine bus driven by a young Federal Security Committee agent. The tall, somewhat surly Yugoslav was Colonel Ivo Mazuranic. His features were Nordic, and he had wavy blond hair and fair skin. However, his wide cheekbones revealed the Slavic blood of his heritage.

Major Peter Selimovic resembled Peter Lorre, the actor, and seemed less cool than his superior officer. The frog-faced Yugoslav agent smiled and shook hands with the Phoenix Force team. The five commandos recited their cover names for the pair.

"We'll be turning off Bulevar Revolucije in a moment and onto Kneza Milosa," Mazuranic announced. "In fact, we'll be driving past the American embassy and the spots where most of the victims of the sniper fell. The gunman could have probably hit the windshield of this car at the distance we're at right now. His marksmanship was quite impressive. You Americans certainly produce some highly skilled killers."

"We do our best," Calvin James said with a shrug, ignoring Mazuranic's sarcasm. "I understand you guys are handling the investigation of the shootings. Have autopsies been performed on Ambassador Woodland and the man who was supposedly Sergeant Frank Cadder?"

"A soldier who your government claims has been missing in action since the Vietnam war," Mazuranic said with a sigh. "We have gotten some information too, you know. I'm not sure if actual autopsies have been conducted, but I would imagine they have been, if simply to determine if Cadder was under the influence of drugs at the time of his shooting spree. I do know a blood sample confirmed that the gunman had the same blood type as that listed on the dead man's dog tags.''

"O positive is one of the most common blood types in the world," James stated. "That doesn't prove much."

"Is there any reason to believe the gunman wasn't Franklin Cadder?" Mazuranic asked.

"We think it's possible he wasn't," Gary Manning answered. "We also think it's possible Cadder may have been converted by the Communists...uh, Soviet, not Yugoslavian."

"Don't worry about that," Selimovic assured the Canadian with a smile. "You'll find our country has little in common with the Soviet Union. Look outside at the traffic. Privately owned automobiles. You don't see many of those in Russia."

There were a number of cars, buses and trucks on the streets, but traffic was light compared to that found in New York, Los Angeles, Rome, London, Tokyo and other major cities. However, compared to the streets of East Berlin, Prague, Moscow and other cities found in other Communist nations, the traffic in Belgrade was heavy.

The people of Belgrade seemed to enjoy more privileges, luxury items, and opportunities for advancement, and a higher standard of living than the citizens of many other Communist cities. Yet Yugoslavia as a whole had problems, including great poverty and ma-

jor economic difficulties due to a massive foreign debt
that extended back to World War II. Considering this,
it was astounding that the country had successfully
resisted Soviet efforts to dominate it. Yugoslavia had
maintained a position of nonalignment while devel-
oping improved diplomatic and trade agreements with
both the West and the East.

"Our form of communism isn't as strict or rigid as
what you'd find in other nations," Selimovic commented, obviously proud of his country. "To be honest, we have a lot of 'creeping capitalism' going on
here. Privately owned businesses, farms and industries do quite well here. A lot of the restaurants and
hotels in Yugoslavia are privately owned."

"We don't have to justify our country's policies to
these fellows," Mazuranic told the major with a hard
stare. "They came here to try to protect American interests in Yugoslavia."

"We're trying to learn the truth about what happened," Manning stated, meeting Mazuranic's hard
gaze without flinching.

"The truth?" The Yugoslav colonel raised his eyebrows. "What truth are you talking about? A truth
that will shift the blame of the sniper incident from the
United States to some other government? The Soviet
Union? Yugoslavia?"

"I've worked in intelligence for quite a long time,"
Yakov Katzenelenbogen began, honestly enough. In
fact, he had worked in the CIA, British SIS, West

German BND, French Sûreté, and had risen to the rank of colonel in the Israeli Mossad. "The truth isn't always the main concern in the world of espionage. In this case, we're trying to find out the truth and decide how best to deal with it."

"So you claim you're not CIA or NSA?" Mazuranic asked.

"We're a bit different from any of those outfits," David McCarter remarked.

"Colonel," Rafael Encizo said. "I'm sure you realize the CIA and NSA already have agents here in Yugoslavia. They wouldn't need to send us if this was the sort of situation those agencies could handle."

"We've been instructed to issue you gentlemen special firearm permits," Selimovic mused. "That's very unusual. Do you really think you'll need such weapons while you're here?"

"We might," Katz said with a shrug. "That will depend on what we find. Frankly, we are going to protect the interests of America and the Western democracies, but that's also in the interest of your country as well. You don't want Yugoslavia to break off relations with the United States or other Western nations any more than we want that to happen."

"Yugoslavia would suffer from losing trade with the U.S. and Western Europe a lot more than those countries would if that happened," Gary Manning added. The Canadian had formerly been executive vice president of a major North American import/export corporation and he knew more than a little about international trade. "Your economy would go right down the tubes if that happened. Yugoslavia can't afford to sever ties with us and you damn sure don't want to be dependent on the Soviets."

"The sniper who opened fire on innocent Yugoslav civilians was identified as an American and fired his rifle from the American embassy," Mazuranic declared. He pointed at the building as they passed it. "*That* embassy, to be exact. Two days ago this street was a battle zone. The Soviets didn't do that—unless you can prove otherwise."

"The KGB could do it," Encizo stated. "Security at most embassies isn't very tight. Have your people checked it out yet?"

"The embassy has closed up tight as a clam," the Yugoslav colonel answered. "Since it's technically on American soil, we can't enter without authorization. Your government hasn't agreed to that yet."

"We'll get authorization," Katz stated. "I don't understand why you seem to resent us, Colonel. Do you really believe the sniper attack was carried out under orders of the United States government?"

"Of course not," Mazuranic said. "That wouldn't make any sense. Your government has nothing to gain by such an action. However, Cadder may have been a CIA operative who was secretly at the embassy and went berserk."

"Cadder was never CIA," Manning told him. "That's been checked out."

"I doubt that they'd admit it if he was," the colonel replied. "Frankly, what's done is done. I don't wish to see my country break off relations with the United States, and I certainly don't want Russian tanks to come rolling into the streets of Belgrade. What I want is simply to have some answers. I want the truth, not just another cover-up. I want some sort of guarantee this won't happen again."

"Believe it or not," Katz replied, "that's pretty much what we want, too. Right now, we don't have any more answers than you do."

"You may not like what they prove to be," Major Selimovic remarked.

"Well," McCarter commented dryly, "*somebody* won't like it, that's for sure."

4

The Federal Security Committee had set up a covert lab section at the Balkan Research Institute in Dunavska, in the northern part of Belgrade. The Danube River, called the Dunav by Yugoslavians, was visible from the windows of the institute. If the Danube had ever been blue, years of factory waste and other pollution had discolored the waters across the eight countries through which the river flows.

Colonel Mazuranic and Major Selimovic had taken Phoenix Force to the research institute, where the bodies of Ambassador Woodland and the alleged sniper had been taken for autopsies. The staff of the American embassy had been told by the Department of State to cooperate with the Yugoslav authorities. Weapons found in the ambassador's office were surrendered to the Security Committee's investigators, who had also obtained dozens of bullets fired during the Belgrade massacre.

Calvin James was invited to participate in the autopsies. The black warrior from Chicago had been a hospital corpsman in the Navy, attached to an elite

Sea, Air and Land team. Like other members of the Seals, James was an expert in small arms, underwater combat, survival skills and hand-to-hand combat. He was also trained to deal with medical emergencies on the battlefield. Wounds from bullets and shrapnel, amputations and surgery under the worst possible conditions were among James's harrowing experiences during his time in the living hell of the Vietnam War.

After he left the Navy, James had continued to study medicine and chemistry on the GI bill at UCLA. He made a drastic career change when he decided to join the San Francisco Police Department and later became a member of the SWAT team. As a cop, James had little need for his medical skills, but since he joined Phoenix Force he'd treated dozens of wounds. He virtually became the unit medic.

James had taken part in several autopsies previously, so he was fully qualified to assist the Yugoslav medical examiners as they began inspecting the corpses from the ambassador's office—inside and out.

On another floor of the institute, Gary Manning was busy in a ballistics lab. The Canadian commando had studied ballistics while attached to the GSG-9 in West Germany. Manning had been part of an antiterrorist squad in his native country. Canada wanted experienced personnel for this job. Although Manning had served as an observer with the Fifth Special Forces in Vietnam, his superiors felt training with the elite

German antiterrorist unit would give him a background in the urban warfare tactics employed by the militant forces that the Canadian government was then most worried about.

Manning had learned a great deal with GSG-9. One of his newfound skills was ballistics identification and evaluation. The Canadian joined Security Committee technicians in studying the bullets and firearms involved in the Belgrade massacre.

By five o'clock in the afternoon, Manning and James joined the others to share the results of their laboratory investigations. The five Phoenix commandos and the two Yugoslav officers gathered in a conference room in the basement of the building.

Food was provided for the visitors. Yugoslav cuisine reflects a variety of different ethnic cultures. The Federal Security Committee set the table with such fare as *japrak*, stuffed cabbage leaves; *prsut*, smoked ham; and *piktije*, jellied duck. Two types of coffee were offered, an Austrian blend flavored with chocolate and a very strong Turkish brew. Yugoslavs have a reputation for enjoying very sweet desserts. In this case the selection consisted of *alva*, nuts and honey; *strukli*, plums stuffed in cheese balls; and a type of sponge cake similar to *guglhupf*, a popular Austrian and German dessert.

"We thought you might be ready for a decent meal," Ivo Mazuranic commented as they sat at the long walnut table. "Anything interesting from the lab tests?"

"Yeah," James began, leafing through data sheets in a folder. "Whoever the sniper was, he *wasn't* Frank Cadder. We brought a copy of the dude's Army 201 file from military personnel records, a copy of his birth certificate and his last known dental X rays. The corpse of the sniper has different fingerprints, the teeth are entirely different and the real Frank Cadder is about five inches shorter than the body I examined."

"Interesting," Mazuranic mused, gently poking a stuffed cabbage with his fork. "Of course, one could say the CIA loaded the files with false information."

"Oh, bleedin' Jesus," McCarter snorted in disgust. "What the hell do we have to do to satisfy you, mate? Bring the son of a bitch back to life and get him to talk to you personally?"

"Please," the Yugoslav colonel began, raising a hand to cut off McCarter. "I'm not saying I believe this, but it is still a notion that others will surely voice. Especially now. A Soviet news team has arrived in Belgrade, headed by none other than Viktor Pasternak. I'm certain you're all familiar with his career in journalism?"

"Pasternak." Gary Manning sighed as he poured himself a cup of thick, black Turkish coffee. "Moscow's version of Walter Cronkite. He speaks excellent English and has appeared on leading news interview programs and talk shows in both the United States and Canada. He claims he's not a mouthpiece for the Kremlin, but he's always supporting Soviet policies—including their actions in Afghanistan and their heavy-handed treatment of political dissidents. He's also constantly criticizing everything done by the U.S. and other democracies.''

"Yeah," Encizo remarked. "Pasternak befriended one of the more leftist talk show hosts back in the States. Their friendship seems based on their mutual belief that the United States shouldn't be in the Persian Gulf, Central America or Grenada. Neither seems to see anything wrong about the Soviets' involvement in any of those areas."

"But you Americans pride yourselves on having the right to criticize your government," Major Selimovic said.

"I don't object to that," Encizo assured him. "American policies have been wrong previously and they will be wrong again. Personally, I feel Washington's support for the contras in Nicaragua is a mistake. Maybe that's just because it reminds me of how the Bay of Pigs fiasco began, and it looks like the same thing is happening all over again. Still, if we're going to criticize that, we ought to criticize the fact the Soviets and the Cubans have set up training bases throughout Nicaragua. They've brought in fighter jets, tanks, other weapons to beef up the Sandinistan armies. They've been doing the same thing in some

African countries for more than twenty years, but there's hardly a mention of this in any form of media back in America. Pasternak sure doesn't bring it up."

"Soviet television is run by the state," Katz remarked, holding a fork between the steel talons of his prosthesis as he ate some jellied duck. He wished more alternatives to ham or pork had been served. "Pasternak is obviously a spokesman for the Kremlin, whether he admits it or not. Colonel Mazuranic's observation is worth heeding. Showing documentation to prove the embassy sniper wasn't Frank Cadder won't impress Pasternak or anyone else determined to use this incident to try to tear down Yugoslav-American relations."

"Anything else from the autopsy?" Major Selimovic asked James.

"Well," the black warrior began, "I can't tell you much about the sniper, except he was a male Caucasian about thirty-five years old. Hair, eyes and features suggest he may have been of Mediterranean descent. Italian, Greek, Slavic, even French. Of course, there are millions of Americans of Mediterranean descent, but the guy's teeth suggest he was probably a European."

"Really?" Mazuranic seemed intrigued.

"We analyzed the metals used for the fillings," James explained. "In America, most tooth fillings are made of gold or cobalt-steel alloy. The sniper's fillings were a chromium alloy with a high nickel content. Pretty unlikely he had an American dentist.''

"Does that mean the gunman was probably a Russian?'' McCarter asked, wishing he had a chilled can of Coca-Cola.

"Nope,'' James answered. "Teeth in Russia are usually filled with stainless steel. I don't think I want any Soviet dentists messing with my teeth, but that's beside the point. What matters is the evidence suggests the sniper wasn't an American or a Soviet agent. Maybe he was a Czech or an East German or something, but I don't think he was from Russia.''

"Interesting,'' Mazuranic said, nodding. "What about the ambassador's suicide?''

"Ambassador Woodland was murdered,'' James answered. "A paraffin test found no traces of cordite on his hands. So either Woodland was wearing gloves when he shot himself and then managed to take off the gloves and destroy them after he put a bullet in his head—or somebody killed him.''

"The sniper?'' Selimovic asked.

"Logical choice,'' James confirmed. "Mr. X fired more than two hundred rounds and probably killed Woodland before he shot himself in the head. The sniper's suicide looks genuine. Woodland was shot through the left temple at close range. The mystery sniper jammed the muzzle of the weapon in his mouth, canted the muzzle up to make sure the bullet would go right through the roof of his mouth into his brain and fired.''

"The bullet taken from the man's brain was also smeared with cyanide," Gary Manning added. "When he committed suicide he went all the way."

"If suicide is going to be the last thing you ever do it makes sense to do it right," McCarter commented.

"Well, I don't know of anyone who did much of anything after he committed suicide," Manning said dryly. "The firearms used were a rather interesting international selection. The sniper rifle was a Spanish CETME, 7.62 mm NATO caliber built on a Spanish Mauser receiver with a scope made in West Germany. The automatic rifle was an Italian 5.56 mm Beretta AR70, rather similar to the FAL assault rifle. The handguns used to kill Woodland and the sniper himself were both French-made MAB 9 mm autoloaders."

"All West European manufacture," Katz mused. "Anyone could have bought them from the right sources."

"Here's the interesting part," Manning continued. "The shell casings from these weapons were also an international mix. French, Spanish, Italian and Czech ammo was used. The Czechoslovakian shell casings seemed to have been altered so the 7.62 × 39 mm ammo could be fired from a 7.62 × 51 mm NATO weapon. Magnified viewing revealed the casings had been reloaded after going through a hell of a beating, the sort of beating a full-auto blow-back weapon can do to a cartridge case. My guess is, somebody got hold of a bunch of used Czech brass casings nobody wanted, and reworked them."

"Very curious," Katz said thoughtfully. "Sounds like whoever did this couldn't afford to spend a great deal of money, and so cut corners on expenses when it came to ammunition."

"Doesn't sound like KGB," Encizo remarked.

"No, it doesn't," Katz agreed. "If the Soviets went to that much trouble to pull off something like this, they wouldn't make mistakes. In fact, they probably would have armed the sniper with American-made weapons and ammunition. This is a very strange set of circumstances."

"What about terrorists?" Manning asked the two Yugoslav officers. "I understand you've had problems with terrorism in the past."

"Unfortunately, that's true," Selimovic admitted. "Yugoslavia, that is the Socialist Federal Republic of Yugoslavia, actually consists of six republics, and two provinces that are autonomous although they are part of the republic of Serbia. Belgrade is located in the heart of Serbia, the largest of the republics...."

"There's no need for a detailed geography lesson, Major," Mazuranic told him. "What matters, gentlemen, is the fact that Serbs and Croatians feuded for centuries before Yugoslavia became a united nation. Hostility still exists. Croatian nationals want to form an independent state, and some militant Croatians have resorted to bombings, hijackings, that sort of thing. But I can't imagine Croatian fanatics managing anything on this level."

"Most of those Croatian extremists are pro-Soviet," Selimovic added. "This leads us to suspect the KGB have been connected with these groups, just as the KGB has been the guiding force behind several terrorist outfits in Western Europe and perhaps in the United States as well. The Croatian radicals want stronger ties with the USSR and they shun the Western democracies. Of course, that's contrary to Yugoslavian policies of nonalignment in either a political or military sense. We don't want to join NATO or the Warsaw Pact. Trade is a different matter. You might say Yugoslavia is almost a Communist version of Switzerland in this regard."

"There were riots among some Albanian nationalists in Kosovo in the spring of 1981," Mazuranic recalled. "That was pretty ugly. Nine people killed and more than two hundred injured."

"Albanians?" James asked with surprise.

"Thousands of Albanians live in Yugoslavia," Mazuranic explained. "Many defected to our country to flee from the dictatorship back home. The Albanian nationalists who stirred up the trouble in '81 were mostly young people who'd never lived in Albania. The radicals wanted Kosovo, a Yugoslavian province in the southeast, along the Albanian border, to become part of Albania."

"That's an insane goal," Selimovic said. "Albania is the most antisocial country on the face of the earth. Their isolationist policies have left them backward, economically crippled and completely out of touch with the rest of the world."

"Rather seems like it," Gary Manning said, his brow knitted in concentration. "I know Albania doesn't have diplomatic relations with the United States, Canada, Great Britain and most other nations. They don't permit anyone from those countries into their country, and journalists are also forbidden. As I recall, Albania has very little trade with other nations."

"It's an absurd little country," Ivo Mazuranic said with an annoyed shrug. "This subject isn't important. It is very unlikely that Albanian nationalists are responsible for the sniper incident at the embassy. The same for Croatian radicals. Frankly, I don't think either gang of terrorists would be capable of something like this. They're hothead fanatics, not clever professional manipulators or trained intelligence agents."

"At this point we can't afford to rule out any possibilities," Katz remarked. "We also have to get more information before we can decide what to do next."

"Any idea how we should do this?" the froglike Major Selimovic asked, his eyes bulging behind the thick lenses of his glasses.

"How about a standard police investigation?" James answered. "Check out the scene of the crime."

"The American embassy?" Mazuranic raised his eyebrows. "We haven't gotten authorization yet, although they've cooperated with us about obtaining material evidence."

"What seems to be the holdup?" Manning asked.

"The chargé d'affaires, who is presently in charge, isn't certain what to do," the colonel answered. "Apparently he's waiting for a new ambassador to arrive and take over. Poor fellow is inexperienced and totally baffled by this crisis."

"Don't worry," Katz assured him. "We'll get authorization to enter the embassy."

"How?" Mazuranic inquired, making a gesture of futility with his hands.

"We'll make a phone call," Katz replied. "What time is it in Washington, D.C.?"

5

Director Haxhi Progen sat behind his desk, reading the personnel file for the fourth time. He had asked for the best man available for the bold mission his newly formed office had begun. The records in his hands left little doubt that he had gotten his wish. Major Argon Vlore appeared to be a perfect choice.

Progen was a veteran intelligence operative of the "old school." In Albania that meant he had been trained by the National Liberation Front, headed by Enver Hoxha, founder of the Communist state of Albania. Progen had been only sixteen when the new government was established in 1946.

He remembered the days when they had looked up to the Soviet Union. Hoxha and Stalin had been Progen's heroes, the warrior gods of world socialism. Progen had believed they would spread Communism across Europe and eventually conquer the entire world, to rule with a utopian brand of socialism in which all men would truly be equal—except, of course, the ruling elite of which Progen planned to be a part.

When Stalin died in 1953, Haxhi Progen wept. He expected the Soviet Union to continue as before. The Khrushchev years proved to be disappointing to Albania. The Russian people had begun to consider Stalin to be a villain, and had made major changes in policy. Progen was disgusted by this. As he saw it, Stalin had led the Soviet Union to victory against the Nazis during World War II. Stalin had stepped into the shoes of Lenin and surpassed the previous Soviet ruler by increasing the influence of Communism throughout the world. Critics claimed Stalin had been a butcher, a mass murderer who had slaughtered thirty million of his own countrymen. Some believed the body count was far greater.

Progen didn't believe these claims, and he would have defended Stalin in any event. World Communism was the new order and an international revolution could not be bloodless. Progen believed the eventual goals of this revolution justified whatever means proved necessary. He believed they were at war with the imperialist, capitalist powers that had oppressed and enslaved the working class.

Although the Soviet Union officially turned its back on Stalinism, Albania continued to model its version of Communism after the doctrines and policies of the late Uncle Joe. The two great Communist powers of 1960, China and Russia, suddenly broke apart over differences of opinion on ideology. Albania sided with China, and the Soviets broke off diplomatic relations and severed all economic and military aid to the small European country. Until Mao died, Red China became Albania's big brother and protector. In 1978, Albania and China broke off relations with each other, as well.

So Albania was pretty much on its own. Reluctantly, it had to establish some trade with other nations just to survive, mostly with other Communist nations, but also with Italy, France, Austria, Turkey and the Netherlands. Albania even reestablished diplomatic relations with its neighbors, Greece and Yugoslavia.

Progen personally hated Yugoslavia. Although Communist, the Yugoslavian government had broken off from the Soviet Cominform in 1948. It dared to spit in the eye of Joseph Stalin. Yugoslavia increasingly resembled the Western nations of Austria, West Germany and Italy. Its brand of Communism had no fire in it, Progen thought with contempt. Yugoslavians no longer cared about revolution. They wanted personal comforts and security. They were a nation of traitors, in Progen's view.

The crowning insult was the incredible number of Albanians—more than 750,000—who fled the country to live in Yugoslavia. Albania, a nation with a suspicious nature, paranoid about other countries and fearful of foreign domination, was very upset about this situation. No one was more outraged or concerned than Haxhi Progen.

Yet there was little Albania could do. Much smaller than Yugoslavia, with a population of just over three million, compared to Yugoslavia's twenty-three and a half million, Albania certainly could not launch any type of military aggression against Yugoslavia. Since the country had effectively isolated itself from the rest of the world, Albania had no allies and could not expect any help. In fact, most nations would probably be delighted if Albanians picked a fight with another country and got their collective asses whipped.

Progen feared one day this would happen, or another power would invade and take control. He considered himself to be a patriot and he wanted Albanian rule to remain within the hands of fellow Albanians and the Albanian Communist Party.

But Albania was two small, too underdeveloped and too poor to exist on its own much longer. There had already been two efforts to overthrow the present government. The first had been an attempted coup from within in 1973. Fifteen senior military officers were later executed for plotting against the government. The second incident had been an armed invasion in 1982, supposedly led by Prince Leka I, son of King Zog, the last monarch of Albania.

Progen feared that these attempts were just the handwriting on the wall. Sooner or later, his precious People's Socialist Republic of Albania would fall. Progen believed there was only one way to save his country from this fate. In the tradition of Stalinism,

Albania had to become the conqueror before it became the conquered.

"COMRADE DIRECTOR," a voice spoke from the door to Progen's office. "I am Argon Vlore."

Progen looked up and smiled. He recognized the man outside his office from photographs in the file folder in his hands. Vlore was a big man, six foot three with lots of muscle. His powerful frame was clad in an army uniform with a paratrooper badge pinned to a breast pocket below several ribbons. Vlore looked like the ultimate fighting man.

Yet his face was bland, his features nondescript. His eyes betrayed nothing. Emotions, intelligence, cunning, self-confidence, none was displayed by Vlore's eyes or facial expression. His was a face that would be lost in a crowd. A very desirable trait for an intelligence operative.

"I am very pleased to meet you, Comrade Major," Progen declared. "Please close the door and come forward."

Vlore obeyed instructions and approached the director's desk. He had heard of Haxhi Progen many times. Progen was highly respected by the members of the National Assembly, the President of the Presidium and the First Secretary. The veteran intelligence officer and longtime party official had been a personal friend of Enver Hoxha himself.

The little gray-haired man who sat behind the big wooden desk did not look much like a legend. Progen wore a dark suit and tie, normally a miserable combination on a hot summer afternoon in Tirane. However, Progen's office was one of the few equipped with air-conditioning. Rank has its privileges. Progen had recently been promoted to director of the newly formed Security Enforcement Council. Vlore knew little about this organization, although he had been transferred from army intelligence to serve in the new council.

"Please be seated," Progen urged. "I have much to talk to you about and you may as well get comfortable."

"Thank you, Comrade," Vlore replied, taking a seat in front of the director's desk.

He glanced about the room. Pictures of Hoxha, Stalin and the present leaders of the government hung on the walls. The Albanian national flag was mounted behind Progen's desk, a red banner with a black two-headed eagle in the center, topped by a gold-rimmed red star.

"Your file is quite remarkable, Major," Progen began, folding his hands on the desktop. "Commando, espionage agent, assassin on occasion. You speak Serbian and Croatian fluently as well as three other languages."

"Serbian and Croatian are very similar," Vlore stated. "The biggest difference is the writing. Serbians use Cyrillic letters while the Croatians use a romanized alphabet.''

"I know," Progen said with a nod. "You were in deep cover in Yugoslavia up until last year. Kosovo region, correct?"

"I spent most of my time there," Vlore confirmed.

"But you are familiar with other parts of Yugoslavia?"

"I know the country quite well, yes," the major admitted.

"You're familiar with Belgrade?"

Vlore nodded. "Does this concern the shooting at the American embassy, Comrade Director?"

"I see you've kept up with current events," Progen said, smiling. "What do you think of this incident?"

"I don't know," Vlore answered. "What am I supposed to think about it?"

"Our greatest enemies are the Yugoslavians and the Americans," Progen stated. "You agree?"

"Of course," Vlore replied. The official party position regarding enemies of the state varied from week to week, but Vlore was not going to argue with Progen.

"Then you appreciate how successful we've been thus far with this mission," the director said smugly.

"*We* did it?" Vlore could not keep the surprise from his features. "I'm afraid I don't understand the reason for this, Director...."

"That should be obvious, Major," Progen said, emitting a sigh of disappointment. "We're creating a conflict within Yugoslavia. That whore nation will soon break off relations with the United States. They'll no longer be getting the support of the American capitalists. Within a year, the other democracies will abandon Yugoslavia. It will become a nation alone. A country torn apart from within and isolated from the rest of the world. A broken nation ready to accept whatever terms we require before offering to assist it."

"I see," Vlore said, although it still did not make much sense to him. "So you already have agents in Belgrade?"

"Of course," Progen confirmed. "They've completed the first part of their mission, but I want you to take charge of the operations personally from now on. You're the best, Major. That's why I need you for this mission. The most important mission you will ever have. The fate of our nation depends on it."

"I'm honored, Comrade Director," Vlore began slowly. "Of course, I'm sure you've considered the possibility that driving away all Western trade and diplomatic relations from Yugoslavia may push that country toward closer ties with the Soviet Union. The Russians would certainly send in advisors, troops and tanks. I think that would put Albania in a very uncomfortable position. I'd guess we'd become a Soviet satellite nation about two days after Yugoslavia became one."

"I've considered that," Progen assured him. "The plan will include isolating Yugoslavia from the Soviets as well as from the democratic states."

"With all respect intended, Comrade Director," Vlore said, "this mission sounds like a very risky gamble with potentially disastrous consequences."

"Are you refusing this assignment?" Progen demanded, his eyes narrowing with anger.

"No, sir," Vlore answered. "I stated a fact. I would never refuse to serve my country, even if it cost me my life."

"I'm relieved to hear that, Major," the director told him. "I'll supply other details to you and explain how to contact your fellow agents in Belgrade. You'll have to leave tonight. I want you across the border and on your way to Belgrade as soon as possible."

"I'd like to say goodbye to my wife," Vlore remarked.

"Don't worry," Progen urged. "I'll have someone do that for you. Now, shall I explain some details?"

"Please," Vlore answered, resisting a desire to object to the mission. He knew this would be a waste of time and possibly an invitation to a firing squad. "I am eager to learn more about this mission."

6

Phoenix Force received permission to enter the American embassy after the chargé d'affaires received a direct order from the President of the United States to cooperate with the five "special agents." The clearance also allowed Colonel Mazuranic to accompany the Phoenix members into the embassy.

Gary Manning, Yakov Katzenelenbogen and Calvin James rode in a government car to the embassy on Kneza Milosa. Rafael Encizo and David McCarter had gone to Croatia with Major Selimovic to check out a rumor that a group of Croatian nationalist extremists might have been involved in the embassy shooting.

"Wonderful," Manning muttered sourly as he peered out the car window at the cluster of cameramen and reporters in front of the embassy. "Just what we don't need."

"I thought these dudes were supposed to be waiting for a press conference with the prime minister this morning," James remarked. "Do they call him a president or a prime minister in Yugoslavia?"

"We have both a president *and* a prime minister," Mazuranic explained. "The prime minister's term of office is four years, and the president is determined every year by an eight-member committee from the Federal Assembly. The journalists and television people are supposed to be at a press conference with the prime minister at city hall, which is some distance from here."

"I think this little group isn't too interested in what the prime minister has to say," Katz remarked as he noticed CCP printed on the side of a hand-held video camera. "Soviet news reporters generally concentrate on building the story to suit the Kremlin's view of the world."

"Yeah," Manning added when he noticed a familiar face among the group. "And look who's the star of this week's show."

Viktor Pasternak stood in front of the other members of the Soviet press corps. Actually, he stood on a box. Pasternak was barely five feet tall. Manning recalled occasions when Pasternak had appeared on American television talk shows or participated in transatlantic televised debates concerning Soviet or American policies. Pasternak had always remained seated, back rigid and head raised high, when he was a guest on a talk show. When he appeared in debates he always remained seated behind a desk, while adopting the same stretched-out pose. The reason for this was now obvious.

Pasternak's round face, weary eyes and broad pouty mouth had become well known to both American and Canadian watchers of television news. Many had noticed that Pasternak wore one of the worst toupees in television history. Yet few would deny that he was an accomplished public speaker. His gestures on camera were always subdued and he never raised his voice in anger, although he'd perfected a passionate stare that added personal conviction to whatever statements he made during a debate or interview. Pasternak's flawless English, laced with occasional Americanisms, made him an ideal representative for the Soviets on TV.

Dressed in dark blue suit and tie despite the summer heat and humidity, the guy didn't seem to mind or even notice the weather. Pasternak was a pro. He held a microphone in one hand and stared into the lens of the camera with the United States embassy in the background.

Manning noticed nine members of Pasternak's crew. Four of them—a cameraman, a male secretary, a young woman with a makeup kit dangling from her neck by a long strap and a fellow who appeared to be a stage director—seemed genuine. The others, all men, didn't really seem to have any work to do. They glanced around frequently and paced the sidewalk during the filming. They also wore jackets, and Manning guessed this was to conceal the weapons they carried.

"Looks like the KGB has supplied Pasternak with personal bodyguards while he's in Belgrade," Katz remarked. The Israeli had come to the same conclusion as Manning about the five Russians.

"Nice to know they care," James commented. "I'm more worried about the cameras. Security is going to be pretty hard to maintain if we wind up on the nine o'clock news on Moscow TV. Wonder what that asshole's yapping about."

"Probably rehashing the embassy shootings and no doubt slipping in some comments about American gangsters," Katz said with a shrug. "That's always been one of his favorite subjects. He works it into conversation as often as possible."

"We sure don't need him talking about us," Manning said. "Isn't there another entrance besides the front gate?"

"Yes," Mazuranic answered, steering the big four-door auto onto a pathway between the American embassy and another official building that was probably another embassy. "There's another gate at the side. Deliveries and such are made there."

The KGB agents watched the car suspiciously. Pasternak himself appeared to take an interest in the passing vehicle. Manning was glad the tinted glass of the government car allowed the passengers to look out without letting outsiders look in. The three Phoenix Force commandos and Colonel Mazuranic didn't look particularly suspicious, unless one noticed the bulge of a pistol in a shoulder holster under each man's jacket. The Phoenix trio all carried 15-round 9 mm pistols of different types, but all were fairly large handguns designed for combat rather than conceal-ment.

Manning and Katz also carried attaché cases con-taining additional weaponry, but no one would real-ize this unless he or she had X-ray vision.

Mazuranic drove the car to the side gate where two marines clad in dress blue uniform with white saucer caps and gloves stood at attention. The sedan came to a halt and Mazuranic, opening the door, noticed Pas-ternak and his crew were still watching. The camera-man next to Pasternak raised his machine to his shoulder as the Russian TV celebrity continued to in-struct him.

"Can we help you, sir?" a marine sergeant in-quired tensely, one hand resting on the white leather button-flap holster on his hip.

The other marine, a lance corporal, also seemed apprehensive. He held an M-16 assault rifle at port arms. The marine guard had plenty of reason to be uptight. First, someone had managed to penetrate se-curity, find the ambassador's office, murder him and shoot down numerous innocent bystanders from the window. Russians were second, now hanging around the embassy like hungry vultures waiting for some-thing to die. The Marine Corps was still smarting from the scandals of alleged misconduct by personnel at the

American embassy in Moscow and it sure as hell did not want another mess in Belgrade.

"The acting ambassador is expecting us, Sergeant," Colonel Mazuranic explained, taking an identification folder from his pocket. "I'm with the Federal Security Committee and these men are special agents from the United States. Unfortunately, they can't get out of the car as long as those Russians have a camera trained on us."

"You can probably do more about chasin' 'em outta here than we can, sir," the sergeant answered. "Believe me, we're not happy about them hangin' around either. But they're not inside the embassy property so we can't do anything unless they climb the fence."

"I understand," Mazuranic said, nodding. "I'll call the police and have them moved. We'll say they're interfering with Yugoslavian national security."

"They won't like that, sir."

"Russians don't much like anything Yugoslavians do," Mazuranic said with a slight smile. "We're rather proud of that."

Without warning, a rifle shot erupted from the corner of Nemanjina and Kneza. Mazuranic instinctively ducked and reached for his M-57 pistol. The two marines reacted in a similar manner and Mazuranic heard movement within the sedan. The three Phoenix pros were also reacting to the gunshot.

The most dramatic reaction was that of the Soviet cameraman with Viktor Pasternak. The man threw his arms upward and tossed his video camera aside. His body fell backward to the sidewalk, a crimson hole in the center of his chest. Pasternak and his KGB partners hit the ground. Then another shot snarled and another Russian convulsed in agony as a bullet punched through flesh and tore into vital organs.

"Get in the back!" Calvin James ordered Mazuranic as he slid behind the steering wheel of the government sedan.

Mazuranic saw the back door of the sedan swing open as James reached for the handle of the front door to yank it shut. The Yugoslav colonel asked no questions. There was no time for that. He darted into the back seat beside Katzenelenbogen. Manning was in the front seat next to James.

"A muzzle-flash came from a car on the corner," Manning stated as he drew a Walther P-5 autoloader from shoulder leather.

James stomped on the gas pedal and the sedan bolted forward. He steered with one hand and reached inside his jacket to draw a Beretta 92-S-B. Placing the big Italian pistol on the seat beside him, James used both hands on the wheel as the sedan sped toward the tan economy car on the corner. It was the type of automobile called a Yugo in the States.

James drove the sedan straight for the Yugo. A figure with a rifle ducked inside the car and, steered by an accomplice, it began moving north up Nemanjina. The sedan chased after the smaller car until a Volkswagen Beetle, or a Yugoslavian-made car similar to the German bug, suddenly blocked the government vehicle.

A young man leaned out the window on the passenger side of the VW, an old Beretta 38/44 Model submachine gun in his fists. Similar in design to the Nazi "Schmeisser" MP-40, the Italian subgun was technically outdated, but deadly. The gunman opened fire and sprayed a wild volley of 9 mm rounds across the windshield and hood of the sedan. Bullets sparked against the steel skin of the sturdy government car. A parabellum slug struck the windshield and chipped glass, cracking the screen.

James and Manning ducked low behind the dashboard. Katz, bowing under the backrest, pushed Mazuranic to the floor. Using the hooks of his artificial arm to pop the latches of his briefcase, the Israeli commando reached inside and removed an Uzi submachine gun with a folding metal stock. Mazuranic's eyes widened with surprise when he saw the Israeli blaster. He hadn't expected Katz to be armed with a submachine gun just to visit an American embassy. If he had been familiar with Phoenix Force, Mazuranic would have known they *always* expected trouble and *always* prepared for it as best as possible.

"Bastards got backup," James rasped, huddled behind the steering wheel, driving the car as best he could in this awkward manner.

"No kidding," Manning said through clenched teeth as he waited for a lull in the enemy fire.

The gunman with the Beretta subgun blasted another volley at the sedan. Bullets skidded against the windshield. The projectiles struck at an oblique angle and failed to penetrate the thick curved glass. The submachine gunner was having trouble hitting anything, and half the rounds he fired sizzled above the sedan. Firing a weapon from a moving vehicle is difficult and even harder when the target is also moving. Twisted awkwardly through the VW window, he was using only one hand to shoot, which made his task even tougher. His position contributed to his problems in trying to blast the hell out of the government vehicle. All things considered, he was not doing a bad job.

But that wasn't good enough when one was pitted against the men of Phoenix Force. When the enemy shooting let up, Gary Manning immediately thrust his right arm out the window on the passenger's side of the sedan, aimed and triggered the Walther P-5 in his fist. The Canadian favored rifles to handguns, but he handled the familiar double-action 9 mm pistol with professionalism and efficiency.

Manning fired three rounds in quick succession. The enemy gunman convulsed from the impact of the slugs that crashed into his upper torso. The Beretta chopper fell from the guy's fingers as his twitching body wriggled through the window. He tumbled to the street, while the fast-moving VW maintained its position between the sedan and the fleeing Yugo.

Traffic coming from the other direction veered as far from the three racing vehicles as possible. A truck loaded with vegetables swung onto the sidewalk and skidded to an awkward halt. The vehicle smashed into the brick wall of a restaurant and shattered a large window. The loading gate broke off the rear of the rig and crates of cabbages, potatoes and other produce spilled onto the pavement.

James saw his chance and took it. He gunned the engine and pulled up beside the enemy VW. The driver of the bug turned and fired a compact Skorpion machine pistol. The burst of 7.65 mm rounds shattered the passenger-side windows of the Volkswagen. The bullets lost most of their power by the time they struck the sedan. One misshapen copper-jacketed slug landed harmlessly on the seat between James and Manning.

The badass from Chicago returned fire with his Beretta pistol. He fired with his left hand, the right still clenched on the steering wheel. James triggered three rounds, blasting away what remained of the glass in the rear window of the passenger side of the enemy vehicle.

The driver of the bug screamed as the rounds tore through the backrest of the front seat and smashed into his spine. In his death throes he turned the steering wheel violently and sent the VW spinning to the left. The car hopped the curb and shot across the sidewalk to nose-dive into the foundation of a library. Thick stone defied charging metal. The impact turned the car into a mangled blob. The driver was thrown forward and his skull smashed into the windshield, cracking it and smearing it with crimson.

"There they are!" Manning shouted, pointing at the tan Yugo, which was still fleeing from the pursuing sedan.

"I see it," James assured his partner, taking the steering wheel in both hands. "Son of a bitch ain't got away yet."

The smaller car turned onto the curved street at Bratstva I Jedinstva. James chased after it as two buses lumbered down the other side of the road. They were approaching the heart of the Belgrade commercial transportation system, the terminuses for both the bus and main railroad networks. The sedan scraped the side of the first bus, then swerved clear of the bulky public vehicles. Screams of alarm and angry horns criticized James's driving.

A woman screamed a string of words as she pointed at the sedan in apparent outrage.

"Aw, gimme a break, lady," James muttered, following the Yugo across a line of railroad tracks.

The Yugo, heading up Karadordeva Avenue alongside a small park, seemed to be moving toward the Sava River, which bisects Belgrade, and perhaps to one of the bridges crossing over to New Belgrade. The government car continued to tail the enemy vehicle.

Manning noticed three heads and shoulders in the windows of the Yugo, but none of the fleeing gunmen attempted to fire on the pursuing sedan. Maybe they were afraid of facing the same fate as that which had befallen the VW backup vehicle, or maybe they had a sinister trick up their figurative sleeve.

Suddenly, the Yugo turned a corner and headed straight for a tractor trailer rig parked on the curb. The big truck seemed ready for the smaller car. The Yugo slowed a bit as it moved up a metal ramp at the rear of the trailer. It rolled inside the gaping belly of the eighteen-wheeler while two figures in overalls and workman's caps stood by the rig.

"Oh, shit!" James exclaimed as one of the men grabbed an M-70 assault rifle from under the trailer.

A Yugoslavian version of the Soviet AK-47, the M-70 was as deadly as its Russian counterpart. The gunman swiftly trained his rifle on the sedan and opened fire. Half a dozen 7.62 mm bullets slammed into the government car. James ducked behind the steering wheel and turned it sharply to the left as shards of glass showered down from the shattered windshield. Manning huddled by the dashboard while Katz and Mazuranic remained pinned down in the back seat.

The sedan hit something solid and jarred to an abrupt, shuddering halt. James glanced up at the thick wooden column towering above the windshield. They had hit a telephone pole. He raised his head and shook bits of glass from his hair. Manning winced as he yanked a splinter of glass from the back of his left hand. He looked carefully out the window.

"Son of a bitch," he rasped as the two guys dressed as workmen closed the doors to the rig, the Yugo safely inside.

The man with the M-70 turned and prepared to blast the sedan with another salvo of automatic fire. Yakov Katzenelenbogen poked the muzzle of his Uzi out the window of a back door and opened fire first. A 3-round burst hit the rifleman full in the chest. The force hurtled him backward into the great metal hull of the trailer. The M-70 clattered on the pavement and the gunman slumped into a seated position near the rear tires of the rig. His head bowed forward as if to examine the trio of bullet holes that leaked fresh blood onto his overalls.

The second workman, disappearing behind the trailer, was no doubt headed for the tractor in front. Smoke belched from the diesel engines as the big rig rolled forward. James put the sedan into reverse and stomped on the gas. The car pulled back onto the street.

"Hang on," James said, talking more to the government car than to its passengers. Using the barrel of his Beretta pistol, he knocked out some remaining chunks of glass from the windshield to get a better view.

He put the car into drive and it shot after the fleeing tractor trailer. The big rig could not match the speed of the sedan and James quickly pulled up along the rear of the trailer. Manning opened his briefcase and sorted through an assortment of C-4 plastic explosives, pencil detonators and blasting caps.

"You got anything in that bag of tricks, man?" James asked tensely. His knuckles were pale as he gripped the steering wheel, and he wondered if his face was equally pale.

"Yeah," Manning confirmed as he took a thick plastic and metal disk from his case. "Try to get closer."

"Try to do it right the first time, Gary," James told him. He realized too late he had called the Canadian by his real first name and not his cover, and Colonel Mazuranic was in the car. *Shit.* "That fucker's big enough to bat us right off the road."

"Right," Manning replied, setting the dial of the timing device on the disk.

James turned the wheel to draw closer to the thick wall of the trailer. The driver of the rig saw the sedan and tried to speed up. It was useless, and the sedan stayed alongside the eighteen-wheeler. The wail of police sirens announced that reinforcements were on their way. Fortunately, traffic was light and most of it had made way for the cop cars and ambulances that were speeding toward the scene.

Holding the disk in his hand, Manning leaned out the window and reached toward the metal hull of the trailer. The rig's driver suddenly turned the wheel.

Manning felt the rush of air as the tractor trailer swung toward the sedan. He ducked back inside the car an instant before the trailer slammed into its side.

The government car was knocked sideways by the blow. James fought the wheel to keep from rolling onto the sidewalk. He took in the terrified faces of a group of school kids with an equally horrified adult escort. They stood on the sidewalk, less than a foot from the out-of-control sedan. Rubber smoked and gears screamed, but James fought the skid. He maneuvered the sedan away from the sidewalk and into the side of the trailer. The four occupants of the smaller vehicle bounced from the second encounter with the rig.

"Not *that* close," Manning remarked, hastily thrusting his arm out the window to jam the disk against the side of the trailer near the twin doors at the rear.

"Shit!" James muttered as he pulled as far away from the trailer as possible without plowing into the children on the sidewalk. "You got 'er?"

"Yeah," Manning answered. His hand was empty, but he soon filled it with his Walther pistol. "Move up, quick!"

James stamped on the gas pedal and the sedan lurched forward, drawing toward the front of the rig.

The magnetic limpet mine exploded, and the trailer doors burst open. Rolling out from the speeding rig, the tan Yugo crashed to the street. The rear bumper crumpled against the pavement and the driverless car flipped over backward on its hood. A screaming figure followed the Yugo and plunged from the threshold headlong into the Yugo's exposed underbelly.

Desperate, the truck driver again swung the trailer into the pursuing car. James surveyed the sidewalk, saw no pedestrians, but tried to fight the skid to continue the chase. This time the force of the blow was too great and the sedan spun out of control over the curb and across the sidewalk. It rolled onto the grassy lawn of the park and slammed into the corner of an unoccupied bench. Wood splintered and the bench split apart.

Another figure, dressed in a windbreaker and baggy pants, appeared at the back of the trailer. Holding on to a leather strap with one hand, the guy fired a Skorpion machine pistol with the other. Katz returned fire with his Uzi. The gunman screamed, lost his grip on the strap and plunged to the pavement, his torso ripped open by parabellum slugs.

There was a roadblock at the next intersection. Two police cars formed a blockade. Three other cars were parked nearby with armed police using the vehicles for cover. The driver of the truck shouted an obscenity in Albanian and the rig plowed into the two patrol cars in its path.

The smaller vehicles were crushed by the weight and force of the big rig, which screeched to a halt. The sudden stop threw the third and last passenger from the rear of the trailer. His body hit the pavement hard, bounced and rolled to a stop, half his bones broken—including his neck.

The police opened fire with submachine guns. The truck's windshield was pulverized. So was the driver's face. Bullets shattered it and turned his brain into lifeless mush. The door on the passenger side opened and a lone figure clad in overalls hopped out. He placed his hands on his head and loudly begged the police not to shoot him.

"That's all of them," Manning announced, opening the door of the sedan. It had been jammed shut by the ramming from the truck, but a hard kick forced it to give way.

"And we got one alive," James added, putting the gears in park. "Everybody okay?"

"I think so," Katz answered, rubbing a bruised shoulder. He turned to Mazuranic. "Colonel?"

"Yes, I'm fine," the Yugoslav officer answered unsteadily.

"So let's see about questioning the prisoner..." Katz began.

He was interrupted by a rifle shot that echoed from somewhere to the south. The surviving enemy agent fell to the ground, his skull shattered by a powerful projectile that had struck him behind the right ear.

"Holy shit!" James exclaimed, sliding behind the sedan for shelter, Beretta pistol in his fist.

"I don't think we need to worry," Manning stated. The Canadian stood upright and gazed at the dozens of buildings in the direction from which the shot had been fired. The sniper could have been in or on top of any one of them. "He's already got the target he wanted."

"But why?" Mazuranic asked numbly.

"You can't question a dead man, Colonel," Katz answered. "And we're right back where we started."

7

Major Argon Vlore lowered the Steyr SSG sniper rifle. He handed the Austrian gun to Ahmed Kastiroti. A heavy-set Albanian with a barrel chest and a large square head, Kastiroti frowned and shook his head. He removed the scope from the rifle and began to disassemble the Steyr.

"Was it necessary, Comrade Major?" he asked softly.

"I wouldn't have killed one of my fellow countrymen otherwise, Lieutenant," Vlore replied grimly. "But that idiot Krrabe is truly responsible for the deaths of our comrades. He was supposed to wait for my command. Instead, he rushed his attack on those Russian television reporters and you saw the results."

"Krrabe probably saw this as a perfect opportunity to attack the Russians and make it appear the Americans did it," Kastiroti said lamely.

"He disobeyed orders," Vlore remarked as he peered through a pair of binoculars at the carnage of wrecked vehicles and human debris.

"Krrabe felt the plan would work," the other Albanian stated. He put the disassembled Steyr into a padded metal case. "It might have worked if the car from the Federal Security Committee hadn't been here."

"I recognize Colonel Mazuranic," Vlore commented, examining through his binoculars the men who emerged from the sedan. "Those three with him are not ordinary agents. Krrabe's people didn't have a chance against them."

"They were very well armed, Comrade Major," Kastiroti agreed.

"Skilled," the Albanian superspy corrected him. "They're not Yugoslavian, either. One of them is a black man. The style of their clothing is difficult to pinpoint, but it seems more American than European."

"A special team of CIA agents?" Kastiroti questioned.

"Perhaps," Vlore said with a shrug. "We'll discuss this later. For now, we'd better get off this rooftop and disappear before the police arrive."

The two Albanian agents hurried down the ladder from the roof to the top floor of the apartment building. Vlore made certain his jacket covered the 9 mm Glock pistol at the small of his back. Like the Steyr sniper gun, the Glock was an Austrian weapon. Vlore trusted Austrian firearms. He believed that Austrians were good at two things only: composing wonderful classical music and inventing fine military hardware.

Kastiroti carried a Chinese Tokarev, a Type 51 left over from the days when China supplied Albania with most of its weapons. Vlore was annoyed that Kastiroti carried the Tokarev. It could be too easily connected with Albania if Kastiroti was captured or killed during the mission. Besides, the Type 51—like the Russian Tokarev it was copied from—fired a 7.62 mm cartridge. Vlore didn't trust anything smaller than a 9 mm cartridge in a handgun to take an opponent down.

Descending the fire stairs to avoid encountering tenants, they soon reached the ground. A taxi waited for them in the alley. The driver was an Albanian "sleeper" agent who had been in Yugoslavia for seven years. No one would suspect a taxi of transporting enemy snipers across Belgrade. They put the case with the Steyr in the trunk and climbed inside the cab.

Moments later, the taxi was headed up Knez Mihailova, toward the Old Belgrade Cathedral and the Serbian Orthodox Museum. The agents would mingle in the crowds of tourists, students and worshipers. The majority of Yugoslavians are Eastern Orthodox or Roman Catholic so the service at the cathedral would be crowded.

Vlore smiled at the irony of hiding in the great Christian church. Albania had officially outlawed religion in 1967 and claimed to be the first atheist state in the world. Of course, a government cannot wipe out religion simply by abolishing it and closing down the mosques, churches and synagogues. Vlore himself was an atheist, but he was aware Ahmed Kastiroti was secretly a devout Sunni Muslim. Almost seventy percent of Albanians still believe in Islam, although its worship had been abolished by the state.

Kastiroti was uncomfortable about entering a Christian house of worship, just as many devout Christians would be reluctant to set foot inside a mosque or synagogue. Vlore didn't share this apprehension. The cathedral was a safe zone and the worshipers inside provided good cover for the two Albanians. They would simply blend in with the crowd, wait a couple of hours and leave with the others.

Considering what had happened at the embassy, Vlore would have a few words to say to Captain Krrabe. He would also have to plan their future strategy with care. He had not wished to be in charge of this operation. In fact, he still regarded it as a mistake. Director Progen had come up with the scheme, but Vlore was stuck with the dirty work. Although he was sure he could accomplish his part of the mission, he doubted things would unfold the way the director intended. Vlore reckoned Yugoslavia would sever ties with America, but that the Soviets would take over the country before Albania could convince the Yugoslavians to give it control.

That was not Vlore's concern. He had his orders and he would carry them out. Let the National Assembly and the party leaders in Tirane handle the mess after Vlore's job was finished. He would not fail. Vlore never failed.

Only one thing worried him. The team of special commandos with Colonel Mazuranic could be a problem. They had to be very special, very dangerous. Vlore's people would try to avoid them if possible. If that proved impractical, then they would have to kill these mysterious warriors. They would have to kill every one of them.

VIKTOR PASTERNAK WAS FURIOUS. The Russian television star had gone to the Soviet embassy to report the shooting of two members of his crew. The Soviet ambassador called the Kremlin and then lodged an official complaint against the United States for criminal behavior and against the Yugoslavians for allowing the incident to happen.

This wasn't enough for Pasternak. He loaded up his crew and KGB bodyguards in a minibus and headed for city hall. The prime minister was still there, and Pasternak wanted to question him on camera about the shootings. He wanted the Yugoslavian head of state to look impotent and embarrassed on film. He wanted to televise the prime minister's stupid face as the man stumbled over his own tongue, unable to assure Soviet visitors or even his fellow countrymen that they would be protected from terrorists and American gangsters in the very capital of Yugoslavia.

Until now, Pasternak had regarded the news story in Belgrade as a more or less standard assignment. He did a lot of work in America and other English-speaking countries where he routinely defended the policies of the Soviet Union and condemned the actions of the host nation. Remarkably, he never had any trouble finding Americans willing to take his side in these debates. It was astounding how many Americans eagerly criticized and condemned the actions of their government, the policies of their leaders and even some of the constitutional rights their nation had been founded upon. The assignment to Belgrade had seemed pretty straightforward compared to the soft-sell propaganda he was accustomed to.

All that changed when two of his men were shot down in the street. Pasternak had known those men for years. He knew their families and on several occasions he had been a guest in their homes. Pasternak had never been in the middle of a shooting gallery before. It had upset and angered him almost as much as seeing two friends killed right in front of him. He wanted somebody's ass for this—preferably an American or Yugoslavian ass. Pasternak wasn't a man of violence, so he intended to nail somebody with what he knew—television.

The minibus drove up Marsala Tita toward the city hall. Its turrets were visible in the distance. The Belgrade city hall had formerly been the king's palace. Symbol of the bourgeoisie, Pasternak thought sourly.

He sat beside a KGB agent named Kerensky, who had been with the Soviet embassy in Belgrade for the past five years. Since he knew the city and spoke Serbo-Croatian fluently, Kerensky had been assigned as Pasternak's interpreter, guide and driver. Like the other KGB agents with the Russian television star, Kerensky had a permit to carry firearms in Belgrade, and the butt of a Makarov pistol jutted from beneath his jacket lapel. Pasternak didn't like guns, but after what had happened that morning, he was glad the KGB men were armed.

"A car is following us, Comrade," Kerensky announced as he glanced in the rearview mirror.

Pasternak turned in his seat to look out the rear window. A small dark blue car was tailing the minibus. The other members of the TV crew looked nervously at Pasternak for reassurance. The three KGB agents in the back of the bus drew their pistols.

"Is it possibly an escort vehicle, Comrade Kerensky?" Pasternak asked hopefully.

"Not from the embassy," the KGB man answered. "It might be a Belgrade police escort or Federal Security. The Yugoslavians should have checked with us before sending an escort, but they're stupid and not terribly cooperative. Besides, they often follow vehicles when they suspect Soviet citizens are inside. They don't trust us. This country is a nation of renegades."

"But they might be terrorists," Pasternak said fearfully.

"It's possible," Kerensky said.

The KGB driver cursed under his breath when he saw two police cars blocking the street ahead. His concern changed to annoyance as he brought the bus to a halt. The police blockade meant the car behind them was probably a police car as well. The damned Yugoslavians were holding up traffic for some idiot reason. Kerensky hated the people of Yugoslavia: Communists who were proud of their capitalism, fence straddlers who refused to support the Soviet policies of worldwide revolution.

The man who approached the minibus was not dressed in a uniform. He was middle-aged, slightly overweight with clipped gray hair and a gentle smile. Kerensky noticed a three-hook prosthesis at the end of the man's right arm.

"What do you want?" Kerensky demanded, asking the stranger in Russian.

"Good day," Yakov Katzenelenbogen answered in Russian with a proper Muskovite accent. "I need to speak with *Gospahdin* Pasternak."

"Who are you?" Pasternak asked. He noticed the stranger called him "Citizen" instead of "Comrade." This suggested the man wasn't a member of the Communist Party. "Why do you want to talk to me?"

"The street isn't the place to discuss this," Katz answered simply. "Please come with me...."

Kerensky suddenly grabbed for his Makarov. Katz reached through the open window of the minibus, and steel hooks clamped around the KGB agent's wrist. Kerensky hadn't been able to draw his weapon. The Russian grimaced with pain as Katz applied pressure.

"A rifle is aimed at this vehicle," Katz warned, still gripping Kerensky's wrist in his prosthesis. His left hand suddenly materialized at the window with a SiG Sauer 9 mm pistol in his fist. "My marksman friend will start shooting if anything goes wrong. So will I. Between the two of us, I doubt anyone in this bus will be alive."

"We'll kill you before we die," one of the agents said.

"Perhaps," Katz answered without a trace of worry in his voice. "But you'll be dead anyway, and it's stupid for us to kill one another. If your driver hadn't reached for a gun this nonsense wouldn't have happened."

"He's breaking my wrist..." Kerensky rasped through clenched teeth.

"Not yet," Katz assured him. He glanced over his shoulder and saw a black commando stare back at him. Calvin James slowly shook his head.

"Stay put, fella," James advised him. "We just wanna talk. You like to talk. I've seen you on TV telling folks how awful America is and how great you Commies in Russia handle everything. You ever go over to Afghanistan and tell those folks how lucky they are to have you guys 'handling' their country?"

"*That's* what you want to talk about?" Pasternak asked, switching to English because it was the language the mysterious gunmen were using.

"No," James answered with an unpleasant smile. "That's just something I wanted to get off my chest, motherfucker."

"Now, let's all put our guns away and talk," Katz urged, still holding Kerensky's wrist with his steel claw. He returned his SiG Sauer to shoulder leather and used his left hand to confiscate Kerensky's Makarov. "Except you, idiot. I'll hold on to your gun until we've finished our conversation."

"You mean this really isn't a kidnapping or blackmail attempt?" Pasternak asked, totally bewildered.

Apparently none of the Russians had noticed that the car that had followed their vehicle stopped behind the minibus. Rafael Encizo and David McCarter emerged from the car and hurried to the rear doors of the minibus. The Cuban warrior removed a short crowbar from his jacket and jammed the chiseled end into the crack between the doors. With a single hard wrench, he broke the latch and a door swung open.

"Freeze or I'll chop the lot of you to pieces," McCarter announced as he pointed an Ingram M-10 machine pistol at the group.

The British ace held the compact, box-shaped blaster in both hands. The Ingram fired close to one thousand rounds per minute. McCarter had modified his weapon to fire about 750 because the slower rate allowed greater control and accuracy. Yet his threat wasn't an idle one, and the KGB didn't have any reason to doubt him.

"Better believe him, man," Encizo added, drawing a Heckler & Koch P-9S autoloader from shoulder leather. "This is one crazy hombre and I'm not much better than he is."

Viktor Pasternak leaned against the passenger door and pushed up the handle. The door did not open.

"Of course not," Katz said with a smile. "This is a form of detente."

8

"I can't believe you're serious about this," Pasternak remarked as he sat at a conference table with Colonel Mazuranic, Major Selimovic and the five men of Phoenix Force. The Russian was leafing through a collection of photographs, fingerprints and dental records. "You want me to take these to the Soviet embassy and ask the KGB to try to identify these people?"

"Those people were our enemies, Mr. Pasternak," Katz explained, lighting a Camel cigarette. "They were also Yugoslavia's enemies, America's enemies and apparently the Soviet Union's enemies, as well."

"I still think the KGB may have killed that cameraman and the other Russian just to throw us off and cast suspicion away from themselves," Major Selimovic declared, eyes narrowed behind the thick lenses of his glasses.

"As the Americans say, up yours," Pasternak replied curtly, holding up a fist with the middle finger erect.

"Is that an obscene gesture?" Selimovic demanded.

"Petar," Colonel Mazuranic said sharply. "Calm down."

"Let's *all* keep our tempers," Gary Manning added, guessing what Mazuranic had told Selimovic. "After all, this is one time when we're all more or less on the same side."

"The KGB isn't above sacrificing the lives of a couple Soviet citizens," Katz commented. "But I don't think it's responsible for this. The KGB would have planned it better. It would have made certain witnesses were present at the shootings, lots of them with cameras."

"The KGB wouldn't have shot your cameraman," Rafael Encizo added, leaning back in a chair and cutting his nails with the four-inch double-edged blade of a Gerber Mark 1 fighting dagger. "It would have wanted him to keep filming so the incident would be on Soviet television as soon as possible. I doubt a KGB agent would have fired from a car and planned a hit so poorly. KGB Morkrie Dela assassins—those in 'wet work'—are very professional."

"You sound as if you're familiar with the KGB," Pasternak remarked, taking a gold-plated cigarette case from the pocket of his well-tailored jacket.

"We read a lot of spy novels," James said dryly.

"I think we've wasted too much time trying to convince this Kremlin bootlicker to cooperate," David

McCarter complained as he paced the floor like an anxious lion in a cage. "Let the Russians fend for themselves. It's obvious the enemy has targeted them as well as the locals. I'll tell you one thing, Pasternak, you're damn lucky *we* stopped you in that minibus instead of the people who are wasting folks around here."

"Your bodyguards weren't too impressive," Encizo said with a shrug. "Guess operating out of the Soviet embassy here has been pretty soft duty. They lost their edge."

"Was there really a rifle aimed at the bus?" the Russian asked suspiciously.

"Yeah," Manning confirmed, pouring a cup of black Turkish coffee. "I had an FAL assault rifle trained on you guys."

"And you would have opened fire if we resisted?" Pasternak demanded. "Pretty aggressive behavior. Of course, that's what one can expect from the American government. Are you fellows CIA or mercenary gangsters hired by the Company?"

"The methods we had to use were extreme, but they were necessary," Katz admitted, offering to light Pasternak's cigarette with a Ronson. "The Soviet embassy had refused to talk to Colonel Mazuranic, and your ambassador threatened to urge his government to sever relations with Yugoslavia. You also refused calls. Apparently, you only wanted to do a hatchet-job story on the way this situation was being handled. We couldn't communicate with you in a civilized manner so we had to use extreme methods. If we really were gangsters, we wouldn't have been so gentle with you."

"He knows it," James said with disgust. "Pasternak wouldn't be bad-mouthin' us like this if he really believed the shit he's coming up with. You know, we could have just kidnapped you and your KGB pals and given you scopalamine. If we questioned you under the influence of truth serum, we'd soon find out if you were responsible for the terrorism in Belgrade."

"Why didn't you?" Pasternak inquired, nervously puffing his cigarette.

"Because we doubt the KGB is involved, and we're trying to get some cooperation," Manning said wearily. "We're also getting tired of repeating ourselves, Pasternak. If you want to whimper, whine and act outraged by the behavior of nasty old capitalists, do it in front of your TV cameras. We don't have time for it."

"All right," the Russian began, glancing down at the photos and files in front of him. "You think the KGB can identify these men?"

"That's what we're hoping," Katz confirmed. "The information before you is all we have on the enemy so far. Descriptions, fingerprints, dental X rays and photographs of dead men. The original embassy sniper wasn't Frank Cadder, although he had dog tags identifying him as such. We think he was a European agent of some sort. Almost certainly a fanatic because he was willing to commit murder and then suicide afterward. Probably he had been individually recruited by a terrorist or intelligence organization specifically for this single mission. The man was probably mentally disabled and too unstable to use as a regular field agent. He might not be on file anywhere.''

"Our office certainly hasn't had any luck," Mazuranic stated. "We tried to identify the man and drew a blank. So did the FBI, CIA and Interpol."

"Or so you claim," Pasternak said dryly.

"I doubted the Americans were innocent when this business began," Mazuranic declared. "After this morning, though, I doubt they are the guilty ones. I was with them when we chased down the enemy gunmen. I saw them take out the bastards. We all nearly got killed together."

"This other file contains information about the gunmen we encountered today," Manning explained, "the sniper who killed your comrades and the men with him, including a backup team that tried to cut us off. Now, the KGB is the largest intelligence network in the world. The Soviet GRU is the second largest. Your people have records and files on individuals none of the other intel organizations even know about. They might be able to identify these characters and tell us who the hell we're up against."

"You mean you have no idea who that might be?" Pasternak asked with surprise.

"All we can do is guess," Katz answered, crushing out his Camel in an ashtray. "Whoever they are, they don't seem to have a big budget. Another reason we don't think this is a KGB operation. An international variety of weapons has been used, which could have been purchased through any European black-market dealer. No clue there. Despite a few rather careless mistakes, they seem to be quite proficient at times, which suggests that professionals are running the operation, but that most of the field agents are either amateurs or inexperienced."

"We thought it might be a terrorist outfit of Croatian nationals, but that seems pretty unlikely now," Major Selimovic commented. "Croatian terrorists are generally pro-Soviet extremists. I doubt they'd shoot at anyone from Mother Russia."

"Mr. Sanchez and I and the major checked out some rumors about Croatian terrorists," McCarter added. "Didn't lead anywhere. Just some loud-mouths bragging about crap they know nothing about."

"Apparently these Croatian crackpots are happy about the embassy sniper incident because they think everybody in Belgrade is a Serbian," Encizo commented. "They don't mind Serbians getting gunned down in the street. The incident also gave the hard-core Marxist-Stalinist types ammunition for their anti-American, anti-West European notions. I don't imagine they'll be all that thrilled when they learn two Soviets were killed today."

"If these men were Croatians, I think we'd have been able to identify at least one of them by now," Mazuranic stated. "The same would hold true for any terrorist group comprising the Albanian nationalists in the southeast, near the border."

"That's if the Albanians were Yugoslavian citizens," Manning said thoughtfully. "But what if they were actually agents from Albania?"

"Albania?" Pasternak scoffed. "That's the most backward and underdeveloped country in Europe. They're isolationists. Albania has enough trouble maintaining its own existence without stirring up trouble in Yugoslavia."

"I'm not so sure about that," Mazuranic replied, turning to Manning. "The Albanian separatist movement, which resulted in bloody riots in 1981, may have been connected with the Tirane government. If so, Albania tried to seize control of the Kosovo region back then. Perhaps now it's trying to seize the entire country."

"Incredible notion, but hardly impossible," Katz commented. "No doubt Albania has a small intelligence network that functions beyond its borders. Its government certainly has a reputation for being rather ruthless at times. Enver Hoxha had quite a few people killed while he was in power in Albania. It's widely believed that Prime Minister Shehu's alleged suicide in 1981 was a cover-up for his assassination after he fell out of favor with Hoxha.''

"Hoxha's been dead for more than three years," Pasternak remarked. "I don't recall any news about Albania becoming more aggressive under the new leadership."

"Not officially or overtly at least," Manning replied. "I'm just saying Albanian agents could be involved. If a small country like Albania wanted to weaken Yugoslavia for future conquest, what better way to do it than try to get Yugoslavia on bad terms with *both* the United States and the Soviet Union?"

"The theory is worth looking into," Katz agreed. He turned toward Pasternak. "What do you say? Will you try to get the KGB to help us untangle this mess, or don't you want to get involved?"

"Fuck him," James snorted. "This dude's no good for anything except playin' propaganda games for the Kremlin. He doesn't give a damn about the truth. His masters in Moscow tell him what to say, think and believe. Let him return to the Soviet embassy and crawl back under whatever rock they've got for him there."

"You're a very hostile personality," Pasternak told James as he gathered up the files. "I'll see what I can do. Colonel Mazuranic, tell your prime minister to expect a call from the Soviet ambassador. I'm certain all talk about severing relations between Yugoslavia and my country will cease, at least for now, after I brief the ambassador about our discussion."

"Thank you, Comrade," Mazuranic said with a nod.

"This had better not be a pack of lies, gentlemen," Viktor Pasternak stated. "Is there anything else, or may I go now?"

"That's it," Katz replied. "We all need to get back to work."

9

The Sava River branches from the Danube and flows through Belgrade. Numerous commercial fishing boats, garbage scows, pleasure crafts and freight vessels travel the Sava every day. Dozens of piers line the coast with hundreds of warehouses to store cargo for transport via the river.

Vlore and Ahmed Kastiroti entered such a warehouse owned by one of their compatriots, an Albanian sleeper agent who had been operating in Yugoslavia for years. Armed sentries at the door immediately recognized Major Vlore and Lieutenant Kastiroti and snapped to attention. Vlore nodded in response and headed into the bay area, passing hundreds of wooden crates that lined the walls. Ahead of him, several Albanian agents sat at a table eating a meal of baked fish and yogurt soup, with tea and *raki*, plum brandy. When Vlore approached, they jumped to their feet.

"Relax," the Albanian special agent told them. "Go easy on the *raki*. I want you to be alert in case anything goes amiss. Where's Captain Krrabe?"

"In his office, Comrade Major," Haxhi Gheg, an Albanian junior officer replied. He was a small dark man who carried a sheathed dagger at the small of his back. Gheg was a knife artist whose blade had claimed many victims.

"Thank you, Lieutenant," Vlore said with a nod. "I want to talk to him alone for a few minutes."

Vlore stepped to the office door, found it unlocked and entered the room. It was small with a bare wooden floor and a plain metal desk. A black telephone and some papers and maps were spread across the desktop. A jacket and a shoulder holster with a Type 54 pistol in leather hung from pegs on the wall.

The sound of water flushing in a toilet bowl drew Vlore's attention toward the bathroom connected to the office. The door opened and Captain Ramiz Krrabe appeared, still buckling his belt and fumbling with the buttons to his trousers. Seeing Vlore, his eyes widened with surprise, and he managed an embarrassed half smile.

"I didn't know you'd returned, Comrade Major," he remarked.

Krrabe was almost as tall as Vlore, with a similar lean, muscular physique. He was also several years younger than Vlore. Ambitious, cocky, impatient for results, Krrabe was the sort who wanted every progress report to include a victory. Vlore realized espionage included few "victories." Most of the time it was enough simply to maintain security while quietly gathering intelligence without carrying out any bold schemes.

"Kastiroti and I just got back," Vlore explained as he stepped closer. "Gheg had told us that you sent a team of men to hit the American embassy. I didn't understand that and I couldn't reach you at the time, so I decided to see the team in action myself."

"You did?" Krrabe asked, slightly nervous.

"Actually, I only saw part of the operation," Vlore continued with a cold smile. "I saw them flee after firing on those Russian journalists led by Viktor Pasternak."

"I know I should have cleared that with you first, Comrade..." Krrabe said lamely.

"Have you turned on the radio, Captain?" Vlore asked, putting his hands on Krrabe's shoulders. "They're talking about it on the news. By the way, the attack team didn't report back to you, did it?"

Krrabe's mouth opened to reply. Instead he groaned, doubled up and reached for his genitals as a terrible burst of pure agony suddenly exploded between his legs.

Vlore had rammed a knee into Krrabe's groin. He stepped aside and swung a hammer-fist stroke between the captain's shoulder blades. The blow knocked Krrabe to all fours and drove the wind from his lungs. Krrabe tasted bile and spit vomit onto the floor, inches from his nose.

"They're all dead, Comrade," Vlore stated in a hard voice as he stood above Krrabe. "You sent them off to that idiot mission and you got them all killed. Eight men, Krrabe. Eight of *our* men. I had to shoot one of them myself to keep him from falling into the hands of the Federal Security Committee...."

Snarling with rage, Krrabe started to rise, attempting a wild punch at Vlore. The major struck first, a quick short punch to Krrabe's chin. The captain returned to the floor. Vlore kicked him in the stomach and watched Krrabe curl into a ball at his feet.

"I'm tempted to kill you," Vlore stated in a conversational manner. "You put this entire mission in jeopardy. I won't stand for that."

"Progen...Progen wants...us to move faster," Krrabe began, hugging his belly as he fought to regain his breath. "The director wants every phase of his mission carried out ahead of schedule...."

"That doesn't mean we act without thinking or planning," Vlore replied gruffly. "I'm aware Progen has given us an absurd time limit for this mission, but from now on there will be no actions taken without my approval. Is that understood?"

"I understand, Comrade," Krrabe assured him, slowly rising. He rubbed his jaw and glared at Vlore. "Is the physical punishment finished or do you intend to thrash me some more?"

"Eight of our people were killed because of your stupidity," Vlore said. "I'd say that deserves a few lumps."

"I'm surprised you're so sensitive about this," Krrabe commented. "This is a large and complex operation, Comrade Major. It is to be expected that we will suffer some casualties. This is a sort of covert war, is it not? People die in wars."

"I realize that," Vlore assured him. "I've killed quite a few people in such covert wars in the past. That's part of the job. The people on the other side who have to die are simply targets. Nothing personal about it."

"That's right," Krrabe agreed.

"But you haven't been doing this as long as I," Vlore protested. "I've learned the only people you really can relate to are the men involved in an operation. The officials who send you on missions are simply using you to accomplish goals of benefit primarily to themselves. You must lie to the people you meet during a mission, so you can never afford to regard them as real human beings. You can never get close to them. You can't even be honest with your family because you can't jeopardize security. All that's left are the men you work with. The men under your command."

"They're expendable, Comrade Major," Krrabe said with a shrug. "Surely you've learned that by now."

"We're *all* expendable," Vlore replied. "I don't intend to lose any men due to carelessness. The next phase of this operation is going to be handled properly. Do you know what was wrong with the way you handled today's incident?"

"I'm certain you'll tell me," Krrabe said sourly.

"Besides rushing into the situation," the major began, "you failed to consider what your people might be up against if things went wrong. You had a small backup team, but the escape route was too complicated. The men didn't have any cover until they reached the tractor trailer rig. That gave the police enough time to cut them off and the commandos with the Federal Security Committee were right on their tail all the way."

"Commandos?" Krrabe frowned. "What commandos?"

"I think they're Americans," Vlore answered. "Some kind of CIA special unit perhaps. They're very good."

"Americans are all cowards..." Krrabe began.

"Don't put too much stock in that Party propaganda," Vlore warned. "Bravery is not limited to any nationality, and neither is cowardice. Whoever I saw with Mazuranic today, they're certainly not cowards. They are very dangerous. I've seen them in action and they're better trained and skilled with weapons than any of our people. With the possible exception of Kastiroti, Gheg and Zog."

"And yourself, of course," Krrabe said, snorting. "You got me off guard, Comrade. I'm not an easy opponent, either."

"I didn't say you were," Vlore assured him.

"Although I'm better with a gun than with my fists," Krrabe insisted, trying to regain some of his ruffled manhood.

"I'm aware you're a top pistol marksman," the major said, recognizing that Krrabe had better be a crack shot since he used a small-caliber Tokarev. "This is all unnecessary, Captain. We'll try to avoid the commandos if possible."

"You're not afraid of them, are you?" Krrabe raised his eyebrows.

"They're not part of our mission," Vlore answered. "I'm taking a team of men to Kosovo tonight."

"You're taking them yourself?" Krrabe asked with a frown.

"I'm going to make certain this is done right," Vlore answered. "I'll command the team."

"We have people in Kosovo," Krrabe commented. "They know the area. Wouldn't it be logical for them to do the job?"

"They've been gathering information for almost a year," Vlore said with annoyance. He felt Krrabe should know better than to ask such questions. "Locals may do the recon for an operation, but outside experts carry out the actual penetration or, in this case,

assassinations. A local may be too quickly identified."

"Of course," Krrabe said with a nod. "So you're
going to kill some people?"

"Strategic elimination," Vlore answered. "That's
what you tried to do today. You may have succeeded
to a degree, but it was flawed. Besides everything else,
you failed to place the blame on the Americans."

"The men fired from behind the embassy," Krrabe
insisted. "They didn't use any weapons that could be
directly traced to Albania and they didn't carry any
identification...."

"That's my point," Vlore said, exasperated. "They
should have been carrying something to identify them
as Americans."

"I didn't think they'd be killed or captured,"
Krrabe said lamely. "Do you intend to allow one or
more men to get killed tonight?"

"I won't dignify that with an answer," Vlore said,
eyes narrowed with controlled anger. "The reason I'm
going to supervise this operation tonight is to make
certain everyone comes back, and that the Americans
take the blame."

"What do you want me to do?" Krrabe asked.
"Stay here and look after the base?"

"Stay here at least," Vlore told him. "Don't leave
and don't contact anyone. I think we've had enough
of your help for a while."

AN AUTONOMOUS PROVINCE within the Yugoslavian republic of Serbia, Kosovo is bordered by the southeastern Yugoslavian republics of Montenegro and Macedonia as well as by Albania. The climate is Mediterranean. There are several rivers and mountain springs in the region. It is excellent farm country with fertile brown soil, and forests of oak, walnut, chestnut and various fruit trees abound.

There are few large cities in Kosovo. Pristina, the unofficial capital of the province, is the center of local commerce and legislation; like most of Kosovo, it is largely populated by Albanian immigrants and Yugoslavians of Albanian descent. While only approximately six percent of the country's entire population are ethnic Albanians, Pristina Albanians are the majority.

Most signs in Pristina are printed in both Albanian and Serbian, and often in Croatian and Macedonian as well. Although Albanian and Croatian are written in a Roman, and Serbian and Macedonian in a Cyrillic alphabet, there is little confusion involved. The Albanian language has little in common with the others, but all the Serbo-Croatian tongues are very similar and most Yugoslavians are familiar with both the romanized and Cyrillic alphabets.

The Albanian influence in Pristina can be seen in the number of mosques in the city and surrounding area. It is not uncommon to see Albanian farmers, dressed in centuries-old traditional garb, bringing horse-drawn wagons of produce to market. Yet, in Pristina automobiles travel cobblestone streets and television antennae jut from numerous rooftops. Pristina is not as modern a city as Belgrade, but it is not lost in the Dark Ages either.

Argon Vlore had been to Kosovo before. He had once been assigned to deep cover within Yugoslavia, and had moved from one republic or province to another. Vlore's previous missions had required him to spend most of his time among Serbians and Croatians, so he wasn't as familiar with Kosovo as were the Albanian agents who had been stationed there for the past two years.

"The best targets for an attack would probably be one of the mosques or the Aurgisca Theater," Zog Carcani explained as he drove the black sedan along Kneza Tocka.

"We don't attack any mosques," said Vlore, sitting in the back seat with Ahmed Kastiroti and Haxhi Gheg. He was aware Kastiroti and probably other members of their team were devout Muslims. "We don't need to butcher a dozen people tonight, Comrade."

"You want this to look like terrorists, correct?" Carcani remarked. A small, blond man with cold reptilian eyes, Carcani didn't seem to care how many locals were killed. The agent had been stationed in Kosovo for almost a year and he obviously resented the locals. "Terrorists kill as many people as possible—"

"I'm in command," Vlore reminded him. Vlore personally objected to killing women and children, and he was certain other team members would feel the same way about full-scale slaughter. Men, regardless of how well trained or disciplined, are apt to rebel against orders they find repulsive. The large number of defections among Soviet troops in Afghanistan was proof of this. "I say the mission will be accomplished as planned."

"Comrade Major," Haxhi Gheg began, thoughtfully tapping the fingertips of his two hands together. "I know these people are Albanians, but I trust you are aware they are also traitors. They betrayed our country, Comrade. They do not deserve our sympathy."

"You can't blame children because their parents brought them across the border," Kastiroti declared. He glared at the slender knife artist. "And what say have women when their fathers or husbands order them to follow the commands of their men? Women are made to bring life, not to fight wars or meddle in the affairs of men."

"Islamic superstition," Carcani snorted from the front seat, keeping his eyes on the road. Headlights cut a path in the darkness. "You are not influenced by this, Major? Religion is emotional rubbish and poison for the minds of the masses."

"Enough," Vlore said sharply. He placed a hand on Kastiroti's shoulder to urge the big Muslim to hold his tongue. "We're soldiers on a covert mission, not terrorists. The purpose of our mission is to create an effect, not a large body count. Mass slaughter of Albanians in Pristina may make our government look suspicious, simply because so many of our people feel the same resentment you two have expressed."

"You're in command, Comrade Major," Carcani commented with a thinly disguised sigh of disappointment. He steered the car onto Trinaest Street and turned into an alley behind a small coffeehouse. "We have arrived, Comrades."

Parking the sedan, he waited behind the wheel as Vlore, Kastiroti and Gheg emerged from the vehicle. All the members of the Albanian hit team wore dark clothing, including hats and gloves. Vlore and Gheg carried rifle cases while Kastiroti held a short crowbar. With the stout iron tool he easily broke the lock on the back door of the coffeehouse.

The trio entered the dark shop and groped past the bins and coffee grinders at the back. The three moved to the front of the shop. Vlore crept to the windows and carefully peered out.

The Aurgisca Theater was directly across the street. Carcani had briefed Vlore about the theater. It was one of the most popular in Pristina because it featured a variety of international motion pictures— Yugoslav, Czech, American, French, Italian, and West

German—all with subtitles in Albanian. The Aurgisca did a lot of business, and Albanian nationals came from all over Yugoslavia to watch films there.

Vlore checked his wristwatch. 9:12. The audience would be leaving the theater in ten or twenty minutes. Kastiroti and Gheg were crouched by the tables and chairs. They were blurred by the shadows, but Vlore, turning, watched them open the rifle cases and assemble the big guns.

The weapons were AR-70 Beretta assault rifles. After hearing Gheg's remarks about Albanians living in Yugoslavia, Vlore wished he had chosen semiautomatic rifles for the hit. Vlore was worried that Gheg, a cold-blooded killing machine, might gun down victims with more zeal than discrimination. This concern was more than a humanitarian aversion to killing women and children. Vlore wanted the hit to appear to be the work of American CIA assassins. Americans are noted for their sense of fair play even during times of war. The Soviet or Albanian government might be willing to believe Americans would willingly slaughter women and children, but the Yugoslavian authorities wouldn't be as quick to believe such atrocities. Since the purpose of the mission was to convince the Yugoslavian government the Americans were enemies, the shootings had to fit the American character.

"Your rifle is assembled, Major," Kastiroti whispered, handing an AR-70 to Vlore.

The Albanian superspy slid a magazine into the weapon and worked the bolt to chamber the first round. Haxhi Gheg had also readied his rifle for action. Vlore knelt beside his men.

"Comrade Gheg," he began in a quiet voice, "I wish to remind you to fire only at male targets who step out of that theater. Fire a few rounds over the heads of the crowd. We're more interested in creating fear and confusion than in a lot of killing."

"That bastard Carcani would have blown up the entire theater," Kastiroti snorted with disgust.

"Don't worry about Carcani," Vlore insisted. "You just watch for any witnesses who might be roaming the street at this hour. Especially the local police."

"Another team of our comrades is supposed to distract the police," Gheg commented. "I hope they've done their job."

"Just concentrate on doing your own," Vlore told him.

Ten minutes crawled by. Crouched by the window, Vlore and Gheg waited for the crowd to emerge. Few automobiles rolled past the coffee shop. It was a quiet night and most Pristina residents had already gone to bed, since most had to report to work at the factories and mills early the next day. A police car passed the shop but didn't even slow down. Apparently, no one suspected what was about to happen.

At last, the theater doors opened and a group of people stepped into the street. Vlore and Gheg readied their weapons.

"Now," Vlore announced grimly and squeezed the trigger of his Italian rifle.

Gheg followed his example and both AR-70s erupted with a murderous fury of full-auto fire. The window exploded as bullets broke through the glass. Twin salvos of 5.56 mm slugs ripped into the crowd. An elderly man in a long coat and hat fell with three bullets in his chest. Two younger men collapsed beside him, blood spouting from wounds in their torsos and necks.

Vlore blasted several rounds into the marquee above the heads of the screaming civilians. Some moviegoers bolted for cover behind a truck parked at the curb. Others hugged the sidewalk or simply ran in blind terror. Gheg tracked a young couple through the sights of his AR-70, and shot them both in the back.

One terrified and disoriented man ran straight for the coffeehouse, obviously unaware he was charging right into the mouth of the bullet-spitting dragon. Vlore cut him down with a 3-round burst. The man's body tumbled lifelessly across the cobblestones as Vlore emptied his weapon's last rounds with a wild volley into the sky.

"That's enough!" he declared. "Let's get out of here!"

Gheg sprayed a final salvo at the helpless civilians sprawled on the sidewalk outside the theater. Bullets sparked against concrete. A 5.56 mm slug split open a man's skull and spilled his brains onto the sidewalk. A woman screamed and rolled onto her back, both hands clasped to her bloodied face. She'd been struck by a ricochet and the bullet, burrowing from the corner of her mouth to the bridge of her nose, had shattered the cartilage. The slug remained lodged in the bloodied glob in the middle of her face.

"Get out!" Vlore insisted as he abandoned his rifle and took two paper wrappers from his pocket. He tossed the wrappers to the floor before following Gheg and Kastiroti to the rear door. They climbed into the sedan and Carcani started the engine. Vlore kept his gloves on as he lit a cigarette. The car sped from the alley. Vlore puffed the cigarette furiously and hurled it from the car window as the sedan bolted up Trinaest and headed for the city limits.

10

"Did you hear about the sniper incident in Pristina last night?" Colonel Mazuranic asked as he joined Phoenix Force in the Federal Security Committee conference room. "Seven killed, nine injured. The police were busy at the site of a fire at a grain mill outside of town. Probably arson to distract them while the killers attacked the patrons of a popular Albanian movie house. The assassins escaped."

"Major Selimovic told us some of the details," Yakov Katzenelenbogen answered. The Phoenix Force commander sat at the table, sipping hot tea and leafing through some of the lab reports of the autopsies and ballistics investigations by the committee, concerning the last encounter with the mysterious enemy. "He said he didn't know if there was any connection between the shooting and the other incidents."

"We believe there is," Mazuranic said, adding yet another file folder to the collection on the table. "The snipers left two Italian-made AR-70 rifles at the coffeehouse. That's the same type of rifle used by the gunman at the American embassy."

"Have your people dusted for prints?" Gary Manning inquired.

"Naturally, but the weapons were clean," the colonel confirmed. "However, the local police did find three clues—two chewing gum wrappers and a cigarette butt, all American brands."

"Clever bastards," David McCarter said with a grunt as he popped open a cold bottle of Coca-Cola.

"So everybody is supposed to believe the CIA or NSA or some other American intelligence outfit killed a bunch of innocent people and were stupid enough to leave incriminating evidence behind," Calvin James said with disgust. "That doesn't sound so goddamn brilliant to me. Smells of a setup, man."

"Most people are going to believe that the United States is obviously guilty, I'm afraid," Rafael Encizo said. "Most people like simple explanations with definite good guys and bad guys. Right now, the United States still looks like the bad guy."

"Colonel?" Manning began, helping himself to a cup of freshly brewed Turkish coffee. "You said the attack was at an *Albanian* movie house in Pristina? That's in Kosovo, right? Isn't that where the riots occurred in 1981 involving Albanian nationals who wanted Kosovo to become part of Albania?"

"Yes," Ivo Mazuranic replied, clapping his hands together. "I understand. You think this supports your theory that Albania is behind this nasty business.

Well, you may be right, my friend. The Albanian government has already made an official announcement concerning last night's shooting spree. They claim it's evidence the Yugoslavian government doesn't care about Albanians living here. They claim that we've been corrupted by our evil allies. Both the United States and the Soviet Union were mentioned. Albania warns that Yugoslavia is coming apart."

"Sounds like you called it right on the money," James said, turning toward Gary Manning. "Any idea how we can prove it?"

"Better yet," Encizo added. "How do we find the assassins?"

"Yes indeed," Selimovic said, a frown enhancing the toadlike appearance of his wide mouth. "That would certainly make this mess much easier to deal with."

Katz lit a Camel cigarette. "Well," he began, "what do we know about the enemy, and what can we assume with probable accuracy about them?"

"This last hit sounds more professional than the previous incidents," David McCarter commented, restlessly pacing the room. "The first shooting at the embassy was flawed. They muffed faking Ambassador Woodland's suicide and they should have at least tried to alter the sniper's fingerprints so that it would have been more difficult to prove he wasn't really Frank Cadder."

"The supervision seems more professional," Encizo agreed. "Let's assume the theory about Albania is right. It does make sense. If Albanian agents crossed the border at Kosovo they'd probably blend right in with the Albanian nationals already in the country, just as illegal aliens from Mexico blend in with the Spanish population in the American Southwest. Okay. Albania doesn't do much trade with other countries. Does it trade with Italy, France, Czechoslovakia or Spain? That's where most of the weapons originated."

"Albania trades with all those nations and several others, including Yugoslavia," Mazuranic said. "In fact, my country trades with dozens of countries. The enemy could have purchased the weapons from some black market source here."

"Of course," Manning agreed. "They wouldn't try to haul all that hardware across the border. Too apt to draw attention to themselves. If many Albanian agents are involved, they'd probably have to use illegal arms dealers, possibly forgers and other local criminals to help them with their mission. One opponent fired a Yugoslavian M-70 assault rifle at us yesterday. That weapon was almost certainly supplied by an illegal gunrunner here in Yugoslavia."

"Yeah," James said with a nod. "If we can find the black marketeers it could lead us to the bastards we're after."

"How does one go about locating such criminals?" Selimovic wondered.

"Get real, man," James groaned, rolling his eyes toward the ceiling.

"I don't understand," the major said, confused. "How am I supposed to 'get real'?"

"I believe it is a slang expression," Mazuranic commented. "But I'm not certain what it means."

"It means, the obvious way you find crooks is by asking the right kind of people where to look," James explained. "You either talk to cops or you talk to other crooks."

"Here in Yugoslavia we try to put most of our criminals in prison," Mazuranic stated.

"So let's find out if you've got anybody locked up in the cooler for dealing in black market guns, forgery or something like that," McCarter said, hiding his exasperation.

"Especially any convicted criminals who've had dealings with radical Albanian groups or extremist separatists of groups such as the Croatian nationals," Manning added.

"Crooked dudes still at large would be better," James told the Yugoslavian officers. "Unless things in this country are a hell of a lot different than just about any place else, the local police probably have a pretty good idea who's involved in major criminal activity, even if they can't legally arrest the sons of bitches."

"Perhaps we can find these criminals," Selimovic began. "But can we get them to cooperate with us?"

"We can be very persuasive when we have to," Katz assured him with a thin smile.

11

The Auto i Biciki, a shop on Dusanova not far from the Belgrade Zoo at Kalemegdan Park, specialized in automobile and bicycle repairs. The shop also sold tools and parts, and generally maintained a healthy supply of such items. Frequently, therefore, crates labeled as tools or parts were delivered to the store.

However, the owner had another source of income that was far more profitable. Ivan Petrovic Cosic was a smuggler and illegal arms merchant. Cosic was probably the biggest black marketeer in Yugoslavia, but the courts had never been able to convict him of anything. The marketeer seldom agreed to meet with any potential customer unless the individual was a foreigner. Cosic didn't trust his fellow Yugoslavians and feared they might be police or federal agents. Anyone who didn't work for Cosic he regarded with suspicion. He had informers within the Belgrade police and probably inside the Federal Security Committee as well.

The Belgrade police commissioner had considered contacting Interpol for assistance in dealing with Cosic and other big-time smugglers. City hall had rejected this because the local political machine did not want to admit it needed outside help. Besides, the Federal Assembly would never agree. Going to Interpol would be regarded as leaning too far toward the Western democracies.

The commissioner of the militia police was eager to help Colonel Mazuranic and didn't object to working with the five mysterious foreign agents. He even supplied them with an interpreter. Inspector Mihailo Krleza spoke English and French as well as Serbian and Croatian. The commissioner vouched for Krleza as a reliable and experienced officer.

Most important from the point of view of Phoenix Force, Inspector Krleza had formerly been a member of an antiterrorist squad in the Yugoslavian Ground Forces during a rash of Croatian nationalist terrorism in the area of Novi Sad, a major city in the northeast province of Vojvodina. Krleza was not well known in Belgrade and there was no reason to believe Cosic or his thugs would recognize him. The inspector could be counted on to keep his head in a crisis, and fight to the last in a life-or-death situation. Furthermore, his identity would not endanger the plan conceived by Phoenix Force to handle Cosic.

MIHAILO KRLEZA DROVE the Volvo up Dusanova toward the Auto i Biciki shop. Early-morning traffic was fairly heavy with people traveling to work. Columns of putrid smoke emitted by industrial chimneys along the coast joined with exhaust fumes created by the motor vehicles. Yugoslavia had acquired one of the less desirable byproducts of industrialization: air pollution.

"I must have passed that little bicycle shop a dozen times in the past," Krleza commented as he steered the Volvo around a tour bus that crawled along the right-hand lane. "I never would have suspected it was a false front for illegal operations."

"Apparently not many people ever paid much attention to it," Gary Manning said. Sitting beside the Belgrade police inspector, the Canadian had a black valise at his feet and a two-way radio in his lap. "That's how Cosic has managed to stay in business so long."

"Yes," Krleza agreed. "I suppose this is true."

Krleza spoke English fluently but his words were devoid of inflection. Krleza was in excess of six feet tall and had a muscular physique. His otherwise pleasant face was unfortunately marred by a misshapen nose that had obviously been broken more than once. He looked more like an ex-professional athlete than a policeman. That was another thing in his favor. Crooks like Cosic develop a sixth sense when it comes to the law. They could be in big trouble if the gangster smelled a cop.

"Kalemegdan Park is farther north," he declared, acting like a tour guide for the benefit of his two passengers. "Very nice place. The zoo is there, also the Military Museum. Lots of history has happened there."

"Are we getting close, mate?" David McCarter asked, a streak of impatience in his voice. The Briton felt the mission had been moving along too slowly and he wanted to see some action soon. "You're sure we haven't already passed the bloody place?"

"It's on this block," Krleza assured him. "We'll be there in another minute or two."

"Okay," Manning said, raising the walkie-talkie to press the transmit button. "Proteus, this is Ulysses. We've nearly reached the end of our journey. Over."

"Read you loud and clear, Ulysses," Katz's voice replied. "Proteus will be ready to change into whatever shape is necessary. Over."

"That's a comfort, Proteus," Manning said. "Over and out."

Katz, Encizo and James were in a minibus driven by one of Mazuranic's men. The Federal Security Committee colonel himself also accompanied the trio of Phoenix pros in the backup vehicle. They carried an assortment of eavesdropping devices, restraints, weapons and emergency medical gear. Proteus could indeed change form. It could become a listening post, makeshift paddy wagon, instant ambulance and traveling hospital or assault vehicle. The rig followed Ulysses, the lead car, careful to remain at least a block behind to avoid drawing attention.

"This is it," Krleza announced as he pulled up in front of a red-brick building with windows covered by heavy dark blue drapes.

Manning glanced up at the plywood carvings that hung from the sign above the door. One depicted a high-wheeled nineteenth-century bicycle, the other a rather boxlike car. The legend Auto i Biciki was printed under the crude symbols. The building seemed innocent from the outside, even dull. Yet they knew the shop was a front for a gangster who had been clever enough to evade arrest for several years. A man who was probably as dangerous and ruthless as he was cunning.

Emerging from the Volvo, Krleza, McCarter and Manning walked to the door of the shop. The Yugoslavian entered first, followed by the two Phoenix Force commandos. The Canadian carried the briefcase in one hand and adjusted a pair of sunglasses perched on his nose with the other. He scanned the store over the tops of the glasses.

It was much as one would imagine such a shop to be. Several bicycles—Yugoslavian, German and French models—were propped up along one wall. Numerous parts for bikes and automobiles, and a variety of tools, were on display on shelves. Nothing seemed suspicious or unusual. A thin, slightly balding man stood behind a counter with a rather unconvincing smile.

"Good day," the man greeted in Serbo-Croatian. "Can I help you?"

"Good day," Krleza answered. "Is Mr. Cosic here?"

Manning and McCarter listened to the conversation, not understanding a word. The man behind the counter glanced at them and nodded. He said something to Krleza and stepped into the back room. The Yugoslavian police inspector turned to the Phoenix pair and whispered to them in French.

"He's going to get Cosic. I told him you were special trade envoys from Paris who had come to Belgrade specifically to meet Ivan Cosic."

"Très bien," Manning replied, answering Krleza in the same language in case there was a listening device in the room. "Hopefully we will find what we need here."

They didn't have to wait long. Ivan Petrovic Cosic stepped from the doorway, accompanied by the thin bald man and two solid-looking guys with stony faces and eyes as hard as marbles. Cosic wasn't difficult to single out from his employees. The others seemed to surround the forty-two-year-old gunrunner and smuggler.

Cosic had an aura of confidence. He was the leader of a pack of wolves, secure and certain of his power within the den of his organization. He had once been a handsome man, but his body was fleshy from a soft life-style and a rich diet. His double chin was working on a third column of flesh and the broken blood vessels in his nose and cheeks suggested he was a bit too fond of strong drink. Yet the flinty quality of his eyes left no doubt that he was still a hard man, accustomed to making decisions and giving orders. His smile was mirthless, arrogant and sneering at lesser beings.

"Bonjour, Monsieur Cosic," Manning greeted with a polite bow. *"Je suis enchanté. Parlez-vous français?"*

"Ne," Cosic answered with a sigh. "Do you speak English? Or German?"

"They both speak English quite well," Krleza announced, speaking English to show he also had mastered the language. "I'm not sure if either speaks German. However, I am their Serbian-French translator, so if there is any problem—"

"Who gave you my name and address?" Cosic addressed the question to Manning and McCarter. "And what do you want?"

"A business associate who deals in the transfer of small arms to private dealers, Monsieur Cosic," Manning answered with a French-Canadian accent. "He used the name Mercante. I believe this is Italian for 'merchant.' *Oui?"* Krleza translated the word quickly, probably out of nervousness.

"I know what a merchant is," Cosic snapped. "But I don't know what your friends from France are talking about. I run a perfectly legal automobile and bicycle repair business. We sell parts, tools and services. We don't sell or handle firearms."

"That's a pity," McCarter said with an exaggerated shrug and a deep sigh of disappointment. "I suppose we must go somewhere else to spend five hundred thousand francs on small arms."

"Five hundred thousand?" Cosic's eyebrows rose. "French francs or Swiss francs?"

"Swiss," Gary Manning answered. "We assumed French francs would be a rather difficult currency to use in Yugoslavia. It is a great deal of money. About seventy-eight million dinars in Yugoslav currency, is it not?"

"Something like that," Cosic commented as he leaned against the counter and stared at Manning and McCarter as if seeing them for the first time. "Why don't you buy guns in France? Surely there are black market dealers there."

"Our group will be working here with some Albanians," Manning answered. "Regular customers of yours, I believe."

"So you're French Communists?" Cosic smiled. "Trying to liberate your own people is too great a chore so you've come to help the Albanians liberate Kosovo Province so the lucky residents there will share the same low standard of living of the People's Socialist Republic of Albania?"

"I don't see any need to discuss details," McCarter said stiffly. "You told us you can't handle any guns anyway."

"I don't know you," Cosic stated. "I never met any of you before. I don't do business with strangers who can't even give me the name of someone I know."

"Pretty exclusive for an auto and bike repair shop," McCarter said with a sly smile.

"Perhaps you would like to see some credentials, Monsieur Cosic," Manning stated as he placed his briefcase on the counter and opened the lid.

One of the musclemen with Cosic reached inside his jacket, but Cosic placed a hand on the man's arm and shook his head. The bodyguard's hand emerged from the jacket. The Phoenix pair noticed this action, and knew the hood hadn't been reaching for a pocket calculator. Both bodyguards were certainly carrying weapons. Cosic and the thin bald man might also be armed. There might even be more hoodlums hiding in the back room.

Cosic stepped closer to examine the contents of the briefcase. He smiled at the stacks of Swiss francs bound together by paper bands. Cosic leafed through the bills of one stack to make certain they weren't rectangular pieces of newspaper placed between genuine francs. He pulled one bill out and examined it closely.

"This seems real," the Yugoslavian gangster announced. "But I don't think you have five hundred thousand francs in this case."

"A hundred thousand," Manning stated. "A down payment to show our goodwill."

"Very nice," Cosic said as he tossed the stack into the case. "You could be police. Interpol perhaps."

"Merde," McCarter snorted. "This man's paranoia is too excessive to reason with. Let's go, Gaston."

"Un instant," Manning urged. "Perhaps Monsieur Cosic would feel safer if he searched for hidden microphones and miniature transmitters."

"They make such devices small enough to be concealed as a skin blemish or hidden inside a shirt pocket," Cosic said with a shrug. "Such a search might be useless. Mico, bring the radio needle out here."

Cosic spoke to the thin bald man. Mico nodded and moved to the back room. He returned with a small metal box with a short antenna and a numbered gauge with a needle. It was a frequency detector, or radio needle as Cosic called it. Mico switched on the device and ran the antenna over Manning's arms and shoulders.

"I notice a bulge under your arm," Cosic announced, staring at the lump in the fabric of Manning's jacket.

"It's a pistol," the Canadian answered.

"Take it out slowly and hand it to Mico," Cosic ordered. "The same goes for your friends. I don't like armed visitors. Your guns will be returned to you when you leave."

He turned to his bodyguards and spoke with them in their native language. Both men drew M-57 autoloading pistols from their jackets. They held the weapons ready as Manning carefully handed his Walther P-5 to Mico. McCarter reluctantly eased a Browning Hi-Power pistol from shoulder leather and surrendered the weapon to Mico. Krleza had not brought a weapon to the meeting.

"Nice guns," Cosic remarked as Mico gave him the pistols. The gangster placed the weapons on the counter and gestured for his men to put their guns away. "Mico's detector did not find any concealed listening devices. We can talk business now."

"It's about time," McCarter said sourly. "What sort of guns can you get for us?"

"Automatic rifles stolen from military factories," Cosic answered as he began counting the money in the valise. "Yugoslavian and Italian weapons are easiest to acquire, but we can get Soviet-made firearms through sources in Bulgaria and some weapons from Austria."

"Some Albanians tell us you've sold them weapons from France and Spain as well," Manning stated.

"We can manage that," Cosic confirmed. He frowned slightly. "These Albanians . . . they are going to move their headquarters out of Belgrade? If this is the same group you're associated with, I don't like them operating within the city or set up so close to my shop."

"I'm afraid we're not familiar with the city," Manning said with a shrug. "It doesn't seem that close to me."

"Too close," Cosic insisted. "They set up along the Sava so they could use the river for transport. I understood they'd be gone by—"

Cosic stopped in midsentence, aware he'd said too much already. He closed the case and tucked the valise under an arm.

"Tell the Albanians to make the deal," he announced. "I'll accept the down payment from you, but I won't do any more business unless I see someone I know."

"What is this?" Manning demanded.

"If you're Interpol you've just given me one hundred thousand francs and you still have no evidence against me," Cosic declared. "If you are who you claim to be, you will have Mercante contact me himself or send someone I know. Tell him to meet me at the alternate rendezvous point."

"Does he know this place?" Manning asked.

"I don't know anyone who calls himself Mercante, but I do know a couple individuals who may have assumed that identity," Cosic stated. "Otherwise, we would not have carried on this conversation as far as we have. It is, however, now over. Goodbye, gentlemen.''

An alarm bell suddenly clattered from the rear of the shop, startling Cosic and his men. Manning and McCarter guessed that someone had gotten impatient and forced the back door of the shop, triggering a burglar alarm.

Krleza dived for the pistols on the counter. Cosic swung the briefcase and clipped him on the side of the head. The bodyguards reached inside their jackets.

McCarter pounced upon the closest gunman and grabbed his elbow to prevent him from producing his pistol. The Briton snaked his other hand around the back of the man's head and snapped his own skull forward to butt the forehead into the bridge of the bodyguard's nose. Then he delivered another quick head butt to his opponent's face and rammed a knee between the gunman's legs. The man groaned and started to fold.

McCarter again yanked the guy's arm from his jacket. The fist appeared clutching the butt of an M-57. The Phoenix pro karate-chopped the thug's wrist and the pistol fell.

The hoodlum snarled, blood streaming from his broken nose. He swung a wild left hook at McCarter's face. The agile former SAS officer ducked under the attacking arm and drove a fist under his opponent's ribs. Another punch to the breastbone staggered the bodyguard. McCarter grabbed the guy's arms, pinning them down, and delivered another head butt to the goon's battered face. The man's head bounced, and recoiled again when McCarter followed up with a powerful right to the point of his chin. The bodyguard sagged from the punch and dropped unconscious to the floor.

The other bodyguard had managed to draw his pistol. Gary Manning seized the man's wrist the instant the gun appeared, and slammed his left fist into the side of the hood's jaw. Then the muscular Canadian grabbed the man's forearm and wrist with his two hands, and smashed the arm across a bent knee. Bone popped in the bodyguard's wrist and the pistol fell to the floor.

As the hoodlum screamed, Manning turned his attention to Ivan Cosic. The gangster boss had slugged Krleza with the briefcase and pushed him away from the counter. Cosic was reaching for one of the pistols from the counter. Mico, the thin bald man, had seized a cut-down pump shotgun from under the counter, and was preparing to work the action.

Shoving the bodyguard forward, Manning charged into Cosic, using the dazed hood as a battering ram. The ringleader gasped as his gut was rammed into the counter. Manning swung a hammerlike fist into the bodyguard's neck and used his own shoulder to bulldoze his opponent between the shoulder blades and crush the stunned man against his employer.

"Bog!" Mico exclaimed as he tried to fire his shotgun at Manning without endangering Cosic.

The Canadian ducked behind the dazed bodyguard, thrust a hand between the man's legs, pushed hard and threw the screaming hoodlum over the counter. Mico, dodging the flying figure, aimed his shotgun at Manning. Cosic, coughing violently, started to straighten up, unintentionally blocking Mico's field of fire.

McCarter scooped up the M-57 pistol that his opponent had dropped. Krleza spotted the other dropped gun and dived to the floor to retrieve it. At the same moment, Major Selimovic and Rafael Encizo appeared at the doorway to the back room. Encizo held a Heckler & Koch MP-5 machine pistol and Selimovic carried an M-56 submachine gun, a Yugoslavian version of the Soviet PPhs 41.

Mico turned toward the two new arrivals. McCarter's M-57 pistol spit a 7.62 mm bullet into Mico's head. Krleza's M-57 put another diminutive bullet between Mico's shoulder blades. Encizo's H&K erupted, and a trio of 9 mm parabellums ripped a diagonal dotted line into Mico's chest. Then Major Selimovic fired his subgun.

The blast drove the bullet-riddled corpse backward into the counter. The unfired shotgun fell from lifeless fingers as the body slid to the floor. Blood seeped from the numerous bullet holes in his flesh. The thin man's shirt turned red as a pool of crimson grew beneath the grisly corpse.

"Everybody okay?" Calvin James asked as he appeared at the front entrance with a Beretta M-12 subgun in his fists.

"Everybody who matters," Gary Manning answered. He had seized Ivan Cosic and pinned the gangster to the counter, his arm twisted in a hammerlock. "One of this guy's employees has been permanently retired, but the other two are just napping."

"This is illegal!" Cosic hissed through clenched teeth. "You have no proof...."

"We have your conversation with our partners on tape," Encizo said, kneeling by an unconscious bodyguard to bind the guy's hands behind his back with plastic riot cuffs. "You checked for microphones and transmitters on their bodies and clothes, but you didn't consider the possibility of a laser microphone."

"What?" Cosic seemed confused.

"It's a high-tech version for long-distance eavesdropping," Manning explained, taking a set of riot cuffs from Encizo to use on Cosic. "A laser beam was bounced off this front windowpane. It transmitted the vibrations in the glass made by every human voice inside."

"That's how we got your remarks on tape," Encizo declared. "You're going to prison, Cosic."

"For a long, long time," McCarter added, returning his Browning pistol to the holster under his arm. "Illegal gunrunning, smuggling, attempted murder, conspiracy to commit murder, aiding and abetting terrorists. Since this is a Communist country you'll probably also face charges for running a business without permission from the government."

"*Sta...*" Cosic began, slipping into his own language for a moment. "What is this for? You people aren't Interpol and you have no reason to go to such lengths just to put me out of business."

"Clever man," Manning remarked as he pulled Cosic around to stare into the gangster's face. "We're going to give you a chance to walk away from this. You can talk to us. Give us information we can use and you'll get to move to another country instead of a prison cell."

"You bastards," Cosic hissed bitterly.

"Well, we try," McCarter assured him.

12

From Cosic, Phoenix Force and the Federal Security Committee learned all about the waterfront stronghold of Albanian nationals along the Sava River. Many shipments of arms and explosives had been delivered to the site. Colonel Ivo Mazuranic contacted the Belgrade building commissioner and soon had a detailed map of the pier, blueprints of the warehouses and a list of the materials used to construct them.

Although different from most Communist countries, Yugoslavia still had things in common with its more repressive counterparts. One of these was government control of all radio and television broadcasts. News of the raid on the Auto i Biciki was easily repressed by the government. Preventing newspaper coverage of the incident was more difficult since there are thirty major newspapers in Yugoslavia with offices in several major cities. However, Phoenix Force needed the news to be covered up for only twelve hours. That would give them enough time to plan and execute a raid on the waterfront lair.

The members of Phoenix Force prepared for battle. They armed themselves with their personal weapons brought from the States. Gary Manning carried an FAL assault rifle in addition to his 9 mm Walther P-5 sidearm and a small backpack with explosives. Katz chose an Uzi submachine gun, SiG Sauer P-226 autoloader and a .380 Beretta as a backup pistol. Calvin James armed himself with an M-16 assault rifle, Beretta 92-S-B autoloader and a G-96 Jet-Aer fighting dagger. David McCarter carried an Ingram M-10 machine pistol, Browning Hi-Power and a Smith & Wesson .38 Special snubnose for backup. Rafael Encizo loaded up his MP-5, a Heckler & Koch 9 mm P9 pistol and a .380 Walther PPK. The Cuban warrior also carried a Cold Steel Tanto fighting knife in a belt sheath and a Gerber Mark 1 boot knife.

They also carried an assortment of grenades, spare magazines for weapons and silencers for firearms. The Security Committee supplied them with flak vests made of lightweight armor. The vests would not stop a high-velocity rifle round at close range, but they might protect the wearer from pistol rounds unless the enemy used "hot loads." The term "bullet-proof" is relative. Any armor heavy enough to stop high-powered rifle rounds would be too heavy to wear in combat.

Colonel Mazuranic, Major Selimovic and Police Inspector Mihailo Krleza accompanied the Phoenix Force team. Mazuranic wanted to get some Padobran-Vojnik commandos to participate in the raid. The paratrooper unit was trained for antiterrorist operations and would be ideal for the mission. However, time was a vital factor and there was no time to spare for getting reinforcements. Cosic was unsure, but he guessed that fifteen to twenty opponents lurked at the waterfront lair. Phoenix Force and its three allies would have to handle them alone.

They arrived at the pier at 2100 hours. The strike unit was divided into three teams. Katz, Manning and Mazuranic took the command team. McCarter, Selimovic and Krleza comprised the second team while Encizo and James handled the third.

Gary Manning peered through the Starlite nightvision scope mounted to his FAL rifle. The green and yellow shapes in the lens were bizarre and ghostly to one unfamiliar with the light-density system of the Starlite, but Manning had used the scope many times before. It transformed the darkest night into a twilight world of oddly tinted objects and creatures.

Two such creatures stood by the front entrance of the warehouse. Manning saw the sentries clearly in the scope. Both men were armed with automatic rifles. Neither appeared to be bored or weary. They didn't speak to each other or smoke cigarettes. These were not cheap hoods hired for their muscle. They were disciplined soldiers.

Another figure patroled the plank walk of the pier. He also carried an automatic rifle slung to his shoulder. He stayed close to a column of crates stacked along the pier. The man gazed out at the Sava, watching the river as if he expected to spot a sea serpent—or an invasion craft.

Manning relayed what he'd seen to Katz, who contacted Encizo and James by walkie-talkie. McCarter's team was also informed of the situation. Radio contact between each group was then severed until the raid was completed. They could not risk a beeping radio giving away an individual's position after the raid began. Phoenix Force and its three Yugoslavian allies advanced in the darkness, closing in on their objective.

HEARING SOMETHING SPLASHING in the water, the sentry near the edge of the pier slowly stepped to the end of the plank walk and peered down at the river. The guard slid the strap of the M-70 rifle from his shoulder and carefully leaned forward. Nearby, an oval-shaped black object rode on the dark surface of the river.

He recognized the object as a small rubber life raft. Two olive-green paddles lay along the rim, and a dark oilcloth covered something on the bottom of the small craft. The sentry pulled a flashlight from his pocket and cast the beam on the raft. The outline of the objects under the oilcloth seemed familiar, but he couldn't identify them for certain.

"Hey," a voice whispered harshly from beneath the pier.

The sentry glanced down and saw a glimmer of light against the lens of a diver's mask staring back at him. He barely glimpsed the curly black hair above the mask or the grim mouth beneath it. A long black tube rose from the water and a two-foot-long projectile, shooting upward, hit the sentry under the chin.

The harpoon pierced the hollow of his jaw, skewered his tongue and stabbed through the roof of his mouth. A lethal dose of cyanide, contained on the tip of the hypodermic-warhead, poisoned the sentry. His body stiffened, twitched violently and plunged over the edge of the pier. He was dead before he hit the water.

Paddling his flippered feet in the water, Rafael Encizo placed the spear gun in the life raft. Calvin James swam over to help Encizo haul the raft to the wooden supports beneath the pier. The veteran Cuban frogman and the ex-Navy Seal handled the task with ease.

James removed the oilcloth, revealing firearms and web belts with holsters and ammo pouches. They towed the raft to a ladder. Encizo climbed onto the rungs and buckled a gun belt around his waist. He slid the strap of his H&K MP-5 onto a shoulder and pulled off his flippers, then ascended the ladder. James took his pistol belt and M-16 rifle and followed the Cuban warrior.

The two sentries at the warehouse had heard the loud splash of the guard's body hitting the river. They turned, surprised and unsure what to do. One man, unslinging his M-70 rifle, moved forward cautiously to investigate. His comrade stayed by the door, ready to get help inside the building if necessary. He was unaware that he was being watched. His head was in the middle of the cross hairs of the Starlite scope on Manning's rifle.

An accomplished marksman and sniper, Manning disliked shooting someone in this cold detached manner. Self-defense was different, easier to justify, easier to live with later. But he did it anyhow—lined up the target, zeroed in and squeezed the trigger. The foot-long silencer attached to the barrel of his FAL assault rifle coughed. He saw the bullet hole in the guard's forehead before the man collapsed.

The other sentry heard the sound and turned, confused and frightened. David McCarter had crept to the rear of the warehouse and moved silently along the shadows behind the disoriented sentry. Clad in black night camouflage uniform, face and hands stained with black camo paint, the Briton blended with the darkness as he moved closer.

The guard didn't see or hear McCarter until it was too late. The Phoenix pro crept behind him, his arms raised, Browning pistol in one fist, the other hand open, palm slightly cupped. The sentry glimpsed something in the corner of an eye and heard air rush forward as McCarter's arms descended like twin battle-axes.

He slammed the butt of his Browning into the side of the guard's skull and simultaneously chopped his other hand into the man's neck. The M-70 rifle dropped from the sentry's fingers and he collapsed unconscious at McCarter's feet. The Briton dragged him behind a nearby stack of crates, and bound and gagged him.

Encizo and James, wearing black rubber wet suits and black sneakers, climbed over the edge of the pier. Unlike the other members of the strike unit, they did not wear flak vests. Meanwhile, Manning, Katz and Mazuranic approached the front of the warehouse while Selimovic and Krleza joined McCarter at the back.

Gary Manning removed a strip of C-4 plastic explosive from his pack and carefully fitted it along the doorframe near the knob. The demolitions expert used only a couple of ounces of the powerful white putty-like substance, enough to blow the door open without tearing up half the building in the process. Aside from the large bay door in front, there was only one other door to the warehouse. The three windows were covered by McCarter, Mazuranic and Krleza.

Katz stood by the door as Manning set the detonator in the C-4. The Israeli, his braced Uzi across the prosthesis attached to his right arm, watched the door in case anyone chose that moment to open it and step outside. Calvin James approached the trio in front while Encizo joined McCarter's group in the rear.

Manning nodded to let his teammates know the explosives were ready. They moved away from the door and around the corner for cover. Manning pressed the button on a radio transmitter the size of a pack of cigarettes. It delivered a high-frequency signal to a receiver in the detonator. The C-4 exploded with a bellow. The lock was shattered and the door snapped off its hinges and flew across the pier.

McCarter yanked the pin from an SAS "flash-bang" grenade and lobbed it through a window. Glass broke and the grenade landed inside the warehouse. Colonel Mazuranic, at the opposite side of the building, tossed another concussion grenade through another window. Both grenades exploded with a single thunderous roar. Debris spit from the doorway and windows. Glass burst from the already broken panes. Screams within the building could barely be heard above the violent boom.

Katz was first through the door. The bay area was a shambles. Stacks of crates had been bowled over by the concussion blasts. Men, who Katz knew were Albanian agents, were sprawled on the floor. Some were unconscious. Others moaned in agony, hands clutched to their heads as blood oozed from shattered eardrums.

Two Albanians, obviously dazed by the concussion grenades, remained on their feet, weapons in hand.

Katz aimed his Uzi at the pair and squeezed the trigger. Two 9 mm parabellums punched into the chest of one man, and he stumbled backward several feet and toppled to the floor. Katz hit the second opponent with a trio of Uzi rounds. The impact literally lifted the Albanian off his feet and threw his blood-streaked form against some crates. His body slumped lifeless to the floor.

Suddenly, a pair of hands rose up and grabbed Katz's Uzi. A dazed Albanian, barely conscious from suffering two ruptured eardrums, had crawled forward while Katz had taken out the two gunmen. The Israeli yanked hard to try to free the Uzi from the man's grasp, but the guy held on with strength born of determination and desperation.

Another figure, apparently not badly injured, headed for Katz. A ribbon of blood trickling from his nostril, he stumbled slightly as he approached, but the fury in his dark eyes revealed he still had plenty of fight left in him. He also had a bayonet in his fist that was aimed at the Israeli's chest.

Katz lashed out a kick at the man holding on to his Uzi. His boot heel smashed into the man's mouth, breaking teeth and rendering the man unconscious. Still, the guy gripped the Uzi, held fast and prevented Katz from firing at his other attacker. Katz released the submachine gun and jumped back to avoid the ruthless bayonet thrust at his chest.

The Albanian knife man snarled and executed a backhand slash at Katz. The bayonet blade raked the Phoenix commander's flak vest but failed to penetrate to his flesh. The Albanian attempted another thrust. Katz dodged the hungry blade and slashed the man's forearm with the hooks of his prosthesis.

Sharp steel points tore bloodied furrows in the killer's flesh. The Albanian screamed as blood seeped through the torn fabric of his sleeve. The bayonet fell to the floor and Katz swung his left fist into the Albanian's face. The enemy agent staggered backward from the blow. Katz drove an uppercut to the man's solar plexus, using the curved portion of his hooks as great steel knuckles.

As the Albanian started to double up from the blow, Katz delivered a left-handed karate chop behind his opponent's ear. The man fell facefirst to the floor. Katz dropped to one knee atop the Albanian's back and, seeing that he was unconscious, finally retrieved his Uzi. Then he glanced about the room for more enemy agents.

When Gary Manning and Calvin James had entered the warehouse, one headed right and the other moved left, both rushing for the cover of the crates. A figure appeared from behind a wooden crate in front of James. The Albanian held a French MAB pistol in both hands and turned toward the badass from Chicago.

James canted the barrel of his M-16 at the gunman and fired from the hip. A trio of 5.56 mm slugs smashed into the guy's face. Several front teeth vanished from his mouth as a rifle bullet performed abrupt dentistry before exiting at the nape of his neck. Two other slugs sheared off the Albanian's nose and burned through his brain, opening the back of his skull.

Another opponent popped up from behind a crate less than three feet away from James. The man did not have a gun. He swung a wooden-handled shovel at James, the heart-shaped blade aimed at the black man's head. James raised his M-16. The tool slammed into the rifle hard and knocked it from James's hands.

"Shit!" the black man rasped as he sidestepped another shovel swipe.

He grabbed the shaft above the blade before his opponent could try again. The Albanian glared back at him, eyes wide with surprise that he had the sense to seize the other end of the spade. Attempting to wrench the tool from the Phoenix pro's grasp, the guy pulled hard. James moved forward with the pull and swiftly swung a high roundhouse kick to his opponent's head.

The Albanian's head recoiled from the blow. Instead of pulling the shovel, James now pushed it with both hands and drove the end of the handle into the other man's abdomen. The Albanian gasped and forced the shovel upward. The handle slipped from his grasp. With a twist of the wrist, James whipped the handle across the Albanian's face.

The black tough guy watched his opponent stagger backward into a wall, blood oozing from his mouth. James tossed the shovel aside. He wouldn't need it to finish off his opponent. The onetime street fighter pivoted and launched a tae kwon do wheel kick to the Albanian's lower abdomen. The back of his heel struck like a sledgehammer. As the enemy agent groaned and started to fold at the middle, James whipped a back fist to the guy's face. A knuckle hit the Albanian right between the eyes and the man's head bounced against the wall. As the Albanian resumed collapsing, James elbowed him solidly under the sternum to ensure he was really unconscious. Finally, watching the Albanian's senseless form slide to the floor, James retrieved his M-16.

COLONEL IVO MAZURANIC, a Model 56 submachine gun in his fists, charged through the doorway. An Albanian killer among the crates, seeing the Security Committee officer, fired on him with a Skorpion machine pistol. Three 7.65 mm slugs raked the colonel's chest. Mazuranic grunted and tumbled to the floor.

Gary Manning spotted the gunman who had shot Mazuranic. He aimed his FAL rifle and squeezed the trigger. A 3-round burst found the Albanian killer. The man's head burst into a halo of blood, brains and skull fragments. His Czech machine pistol clattered to the floor and his mangled body fell from view.

"Colonel?" Manning knelt beside Mazuranic. The Yugoslavian intelligence officer lay on his back, breathing heavily, a startled expression on his face. "How bad is it, Colonel?"

"It feels as if someone with fists of stone punched me in the chest," Mazuranic answered, moving a hand over the dents in his flak vest. "But I'm all right. None of the bullets got through the armor."

"Stay down and catch your breath," Manning advised. "Looks like we've beaten this lot, anyway."

As if to prove Manning wrong, three Albanians appeared with M-70 rifles and M-56 subguns at the back of the bay. McCarter and Selimovic entered the building as a wave of 7.62 mm bullets streaked from the enemies' position. The Briton hit the floor and slid to cover behind a fallen crate. Katz scrambled to shelter behind a forklift truck. Selimovic rushed to the cover of a storage bin and the others simply ducked behind the nearest crates.

"You were saying?" Mazuranic asked dryly.

"Well, maybe we're not quite finished after all," Manning answered, easing the barrel of his FAL around the corner of a crate.

He fired two short bursts in the general direction of the enemy snipers, intended to keep them occupied for a moment so the others could move into position or advance.

McCarter dashed to a crate closer to the enemy, firing a quick burst with his Ingram M-10 at the Albanian gunsels as he moved from cover to cover. Selimovic followed the Briton's example and darted from the storage bin to a stack of crates. James fired a salvo of M-16 rounds to keep the Albanians busy while Selimovic moved.

Katz crept alongside the forklift to the operator's seat. He noticed the key in the ignition. The Israeli pulled the P-226 pistol from his shoulder holster and thrust it into his belt. Then he removed his leather shoulder holster rig, tied one end to the steel upright part of the load-carry forks. He used the hooks of his artificial arm to knot the straps.

The Albanian gunmen fired. Several bullets rang against the steel frame of the forklift. Crouching, Katz waited for the shooting to let up. The other Phoenix fighters and the two Yugoslavians fired back, which pinned down the enemy long enough for Katz to turn the ignition key and start the forklift engine.

The Israeli turned the steering wheel to aim the forklift at the enemy. He tied the other end of the leather holster strap to the wheel to lock it in place as the forklift started to roll forward. Katz hopped off the contraption and, landing on the floor, rolled for cover behind some crates. Two 7.62 mm slugs dug into the floor near his tumbling form but no bullets struck flesh.

The forklift lumbered forward awkwardly and crashed into the crates used by the enemy gunmen. Two of them tried to run to another set of crates. David McCarter trained his Ingram on the pair and opened fire. Parabellums ripped one from belly button to breastbone. The man whirled and fell, barely twitching as life seeped away. McCarter nailed the second with another burst of 9 mm slugs. The bullets struck high in the chest and the left shoulder.

The force of the bullets spun the dazed gunsel around. The M56 subgun flew from his fingers. He staggered forward. Major Selimovic fired his own M-56 and blasted a trio of 7.62 mm rounds into the man's chest, finishing the job the Ingram slugs had started.

A third Albanian triggerman had ducked back into a corner to evade the forklift. The big steel forks crashed into two crates and pushed them against the wall, shattering them on impact. The forks actually punched through the wooden wall before the machine finally came to a halt. The engine continued to run and the wheels to spin as the forklift truck pushed against the wall as if trying to tear it down.

The Albanian gunman was almost crushed by the crates that tumbled down around him. Confused, frightened and desperate, he could barely see past the boxes that had fallen into the corner. He had little room to move. It seemed he was trapped in the corner and could do nothing but wait for the mysterious raiders to find him and finish him off.

Then he saw the broken window beside him. The Albanian grabbed the sill, hauled himself up and wiggled through the window. He slid outside and dropped to the ground below. The cool night air was a great relief. The Albanian closed his eyes and gratefully inhaled the fresh sea-scented air. He smiled. He had escaped. He was safe.

"Hold it right there." Rafael Encizo jammed the muzzle of his H&K MP-5 into the back of the Albanian's head. "You may not understand what I say, but you'd better understand what this means."

He jabbed the muzzle harder. The Albanian slowly raised his hands to shoulder level in surrender. Suddenly he pivoted and attempted to grab Encizo's weapon. His hands seized nothing but air.

Encizo, who had moved his MP-5 the instant the Albanian began to turn, was familiar with the tactic his opponent had attempted. It's taught in military hand-to-hand manuals all over the world, but it seldom works if the other guy is watching for it.

The Cuban-American stabbed the barrel of his H&K subgun into the Albanian's solar plexus. The startled agent gasped in agony and clutched his abdomen. Encizo smashed the steel frame of his MP-5 into the point of his opponent's chin. The Albanian crashed to the plank walk at Encizo's feet, where he moaned softly and gingerly touched his aching jawbone.

"At least you understood that," Encizo remarked with a shrug.

MAJOR SELIMOVIC SAW the Albanian henchman slither out the window. He broke cover to charge toward the window, literally hoping to put a couple of bullets up the man's ass before the Albanian could escape. He was aware Encizo and Krleza were stationed outside to handle any enemies who made it free in this manner, but Selimovic wanted to be certain the bastard did not get away.

"No!" Katz yelled at the Yugoslavian officer. "Get back!"

The warning came too late. A pistol snarled from the doorway of the office. Major Selimovic stopped in his tracks and stumbled backward. He started to raise his hands to his toadlike face, stopped in midaction and fell. The left lens of his eyeglasses had been shattered by the bullet, which also gouged through his eye socket and drilled into his brain.

"Dirty bleeder," McCarter growled as he fired a salvo of Ingram rounds at the office door.

Bullets chipped wood from the door and surrounding frame. McCarter jogged forward, dived to the floor and slid to a pile of crates less than two yards from the door. Having exhausted the ammo in the 32-round magazine of the Ingram machine pistol, the Briton did not take time to reload. He placed the M-10 on the floor and drew his Browning Hi-Power instead.

An arm extended from the doorway, a Chinese Tokarev pistol in its fist. McCarter held his Browning in both hands and aimed around the crates. The so-called weaver combat stance was second nature to the British ace. McCarter had been a contender for the Olympic pistol marksmanship team in Great Britain in the 1970s. He didn't need a mansize target to be able to hit it at six feet.

He triggered the Browning and the pistol roared. The fist holding the Tokarev vanished. The Chinese pistol hopped into the air and fell to the floor. Inside the office, a voice cried out in pain. Less than eight seconds later, Captain Ramiz Krrabe staggered across the threshold, his hands raised overhead. A handkerchief was bound around one hand. Blood streamed from the white cloth and streaked down the upraised arm.

"Come here, you bastard," McCarter instructed, pointing his Browning at the Albanian officer's chest. "Keep your bloody hands up...the bloody hand and the other one, too, you filthy little sod."

"He may not understand English," Katz said as he approached McCarter and the prisoner. "We'll have Mazuranic talk to him. I think he's the last one of these scum, but we'll check the office to make sure."

"Maybe we've just wrapped up our mission," the Briton remarked, still watching Krrabe like a hungry hawk.

"Maybe," Katz replied. But his instincts told him their job was far from finished.

13

New Belgrade—or Novi Beograd—is a triumph of twentieth-century technology. Formerly swampland, across the Sava River from Belgrade, the area has been transformed into an extension of the centuries-old city. Buildings stand on ground that had not been intended by nature to hold such mighty structures. Many criticized the big stone sculptures near the Modern Art Museum in New Belgrade. The statues resemble giant, mutant mushrooms in stone. Yet in a sense these sculptures symbolize the achievement of the area: man defying nature and winning.

Yakov Katzenelenbogen and Colonel Ivo Mazuranic waited in the empty concert hall at the Sava Center, the largest cultural complex in New Belgrade. The hall was dimly lit and as quiet as a mausoleum. The backrests of the rows of empty seats resembled headstones in the darkness. Every sound was magnified and echoed within the concert hall.

Several long dull minutes passed before a door opened and a man dressed in a dark blue suit entered the hall. He carried a briefcase and walked with a confident stride and a straight posture. His face was round and smiled easily and the features were ordinary and pleasant. One might have guessed him to be a banker or businessman in his late thirties or early forties. He was not.

"Good afternoon, gentlemen," he addressed Katz and Mazuranic in English as he approached. "Have you seen Viktor?"

"Didn't Viktor send you?" Katz replied with the prearranged password.

"In fact he did," the stranger confirmed and nodded at the pair. "You can call me Boris if you like. It isn't my name, of course, but no one uses his real name in my line of work."

He removed a passport and embassy identification folder. It was written in Russian Cyrillic letters. Mazuranic didn't read Russian, but he pretended to study the papers with care. Katz was fluent in Russian and could read the language with ease, yet he barely glanced at the ID Boris showed them. He was convinced Boris was a KGB case officer from the Soviet embassy and that was all that really mattered.

"Please join us, Boris," Mazuranic offered.

"Thank you, Colonel," the Russian said as he sat next to the Yugoslavian intelligence officer. "Of course, I know you're Colonel Mazuranic of the Federal Security Committee. No state secret there. I don't know your friend by name, but I think I may have read some reports concerning some of his activities in the past. Reports about five mysterious commando types who keep popping up all over the world. The last concerned an affair in Finland, as I recall.''

''Finland isn't the reason for this meeting,'' Katz told him. ''I can give you a false name if you like, but that isn't very important right now either. A problem has occurred that concerns the interests of your nation as much as it does mine or that of Colonel Mazuranic.''

''That's what Viktor Pasternak claims,'' Boris said with a smile. ''You people frightened the daylights out of that poor television announcer. He's not accustomed to having guns pointed at him or being carried off to secret meetings to have strange agents from capitalist countries use him as a go-between for the KGB.''

''We added a bit of excitement to Mister Pasternak's life,'' Katz replied. ''He wasn't harmed and neither were any of your KGB comrades who were with him when we first contacted him.''

''None of my KGB comrades were harmed on *this* occasion,'' Boris commented. ''You realize of course, Moscow considers you and your elite team of commandos to be among our most serious enemies. You've caused quite a bit of trouble for the KGB in the past and there are some doubts we can trust you now.''

''You can trust us to do what's in the best interest of the Western democracies and we can trust the KGB to do the same for the interests of the Soviet Union,''

Katz answered with a shrug. "Some time ago, your country was faced with an embarrassment. The sort of embarrassment that could have gotten millions of people killed. The interests of your side were identical with those of our side. We called a truce and actually worked with the KGB in order to accomplish our common goal. The situation is much the same now. We both share a common enemy, Boris. Do we call a truce and work together, or do we go our separate ways?"

"We have a truce," Boris assured him. "Although Moscow did find it difficult to believe Albania could be responsible for everything that's happened over the past week. Albania isn't exactly the sort of country one stays up worrying about."

"I'm sure you know about our raid on the waterfront headquarters," Mazuranic began. "The building was filled with Albanian agents. Most of them were killed in the battle. A comrade and close friend of mine was also killed. However, we took several prisoners and questioned them under the influence of scopolamine. There's no doubt Albania is responsible for all the tragedy and tension Belgrade has suffered in the past few days."

"Albania may not be responsible," Katz added. "But Director Progen of the Albanian Security Enforcement Council certainly is."

"That's why Moscow thinks this story may be true," Boris explained as he opened his briefcase.

"Haxhi Progen is an old-line Albanian Communist Party leader of the Hoxha school of socialism. A political fanatic and an extremist by anyone's definition. The notion of setting America against the Soviets and both sides against Yugoslavia is just the sort of lunacy Progen would come up with. Yet, the most convincing evidence you told us was the name Argon Vlore."

"The Albanian case officer in charge of operations here in Yugoslavia," Katz said with a nod. "We got that name from a man named Krrabe, who was more or less second in command. Apparently there was some friction between Vlore and Krrabe and they didn't get along very well. Krrabe ordered the strike on Pasternak's TV crew, by the way. Doesn't seem terribly professional to me."

"The same can't be said about Vlore," Boris warned as he handed Mazuranic two sets of file folders. "Here's some information on Vlore as well as on Progen and a couple other names you gave us. The file on Vlore isn't very thick. Even the KGB doesn't know much about what goes on within Albanian intelligence, but what we do know about Vlore is impressive. We went to the trouble of translating this data into both Serbian and English."

"How considerate," Katz remarked. "Thank you."

"You shared information with us first," Boris said with a tight smile. "My government is frankly relieved that this unpleasantness doesn't involve either the United States or Yugoslavia. This isn't a convenient time for the Soviet Union to develop any major new international problems. We've got our hands full with some problems of our own."

"Those Afghan rebels just don't seem to appreciate the Soviet occupation of their country," Katz said dryly.

"Let's not bring that up, gentlemen," Boris urged. "I believe we've concluded our business. The Soviet Union will not be breaking relations with Yugoslavia and there will be no more public criticism by Soviet officials of the United States embassy in Belgrade."

"I don't suppose Moscow will retract the earlier criticism, and admit it was based on false information?" Katz asked.

"Don't be silly," Boris said with a laugh. "Politicians never like to admit they were wrong. That is true whether we're talking about Moscow or Washington. We'll just let the incident blow over. Within a week, no one will remember it ever happened. That's the beauty of world events. Things happen so quickly it is easy to bury a relatively minor incident among the tidal wave of news that follows. The Albanians turned against us Soviets after Stalin died, so we don't really mind if they catch all the hell when this is over. Oh, I feel I should add that officially the Soviet Union and the KGB know nothing about this meeting or the events that led up to it. We will, of course, deny any involvement in this whatsoever. The documents I gave you have no Soviet or embassy seals. Since they aren't printed in Russian or even on Russian paper, there's no evidence to prove we supplied you with them.''

"Naturally," Katz mused. "We mustn't let the rest of the world know we can actually cooperate and reason together from time to time. What a dreadful scandal that would be.''

"You know how the game is played," Boris said as he started to rise. "It doesn't always make sense, but the rules still apply. Take comfort in the fact that as long as we have a truce going, the KGB won't kill you and your friends. After all, you're carrying out a mission that can be to our benefit, if you're successful. Besides, Vlore might take care of you and your group for us.''

"Don't count on that," Katz replied.

"Doesn't matter anyway," Boris stated as he closed his briefcase. "If you survive now, the KGB will deal with you sometime in the future. No one ever escapes when the Sword and Shield mark them for death. Personally, I don't find you to be some sort of monster. I'm sure your friends are basically decent sorts as well. However, you have killed a number of my comrades in the past, so I won't shed any tears when your group is finally exterminated.''

"Not while they're in Yugoslavia," Mazuranic said in a hard voice. "There's already been too much bloodshed, and it may not be over yet. If the KGB decides to contribute to the butchery by killing men who are here to help us handle this situation, I shall personally see to it things are very unpleasant for every Soviet citizen in my country—legally and otherwise. You'd be surprised how many KGB agents we know about but have chosen to leave alone for now. All that could change if your people decide to carry out a vendetta in Yugoslavia."

"Don't worry," Boris assured him. "We have a truce. Just make certain they don't stay in Yugoslavia after their work here is done. No need to tempt the Kremlin. If that's everything, I must be going."

"It's been charming," Katz said dryly.

The KGB officer left the concert hall. Colonel Mazuranic sighed and tucked the files under his arm. Katz took out his Camels and fired up a cigarette. The hall was once again silent, brooding and still.

"I hope there's something here that can help us," the Yugoslavian officer remarked. "Krrabe doesn't have any idea where Vlore might be. He may even have headed back across the border to Albania."

"Perhaps," Katz said thoughtfully. "Let's get back to your headquarters and talk about this with the others. Then we can figure out what to do next."

KATZ AND MAZURANIC MET with the other four members of Phoenix Force at the Security Committee's conference room. They examined the KGB files on Argon Vlore. Boris had been right. The information was impressive.

"So Vlore speaks at least four languages fluently, he's an expert in hand-to-hand combat, small arms, infiltration, assassination, disguise and tactics," Rafael Encizo said, leaning back in his chair. "Just another run-of-the-mill brilliant superspy."

"Well, Vlore must know his mission has gone sour," Calvin James remarked. "You can bet your ass he knows what happened to the base at the waterfront. Could be he decided the best thing to do would be cut his losses, said 'That's the way the covert cookie crumbles,' and boogied back to Albania before he lost any more men."

"I'm not so sure about that," McCarter said, sipping chilled Coca-Cola. "The file says this bloke has never failed a mission. Never ran out on a job until it was finished. I don't think he'll leave as long as he thinks there still might be a chance of salvaging his mission."

"What the fuck is left to salvage?" James asked, rolling his eyes toward the ceiling. "We found out the Albanians are responsible for the embassy shooting, the attack on Pasternak's TV crew and probably the massacre in Pristina. There's nothing left for Vlore to do now but try to save his own ass."

"He won't do that by returning to Albania," Katz declared. "If Vlore was CIA, British Secret Service, Mossad, BND, even KGB, he could go home and probably get some degree of recognition for what he accomplished instead of just punishment for what went wrong. Most intelligence outfits don't expect every mission to be a success, especially one that's extremely ambitious. They wouldn't be inclined to execute an agent for fumbling a mission. A man with Vlore's skills and experience would be considered a valuable asset. Most intel groups would want to keep him alive, but Director Progen will probably put Vlore before a firing squad or throw him in prison to rot if he returns to Albania now."

"Vlore might choose to defect," Mazuranic stated. "Yugoslavia has a much higher standard of living than Albania. I know I'm biased in favor of my country, but I think you'll agree we have better technology, medical treatment, leisure activities and goods and services. Vlore must realize we would welcome a man with his abilities and we'd be willing to overlook his involvement in this business. The man was just following orders."

"He won't defect," Gary Manning declared. "Vlore is a patriot who had the misfortune of being born in a country that's exploited his love for his homeland. Besides, he knows what Yugoslavia is like since he's been here before. If he wanted to defect to find a cushy life here, he would have done it already. I figure Vlore is totally dedicated to carrying out his missions. Duty is a religion for him. I doubt if he thinks much of the government of Albania and he probably figured the current mission was a harebrained scheme from the start. Still, he'll carry out his duty because that's what his life has always been. Defecting would be unthinkable and returning to Albania a failure would be fatal. I don't think he's given up and I don't think he's left the country, either."

"Those are a lot of assumptions to make about a man from what little information the KGB gave us about him," Mazuranic remarked.

"There's more here if you consider what the information means instead of simply viewing it as dry facts," the Canadian insisted. "Vlore's skills are extraordinary. That means his dedication in acquiring them was far greater than normal. He's never failed a mission and that means he won't settle for less than success. Not just because he's afraid of his leaders, but because that's the kind of man he is."

"Sort of like us," James commented.

"Exactly," Manning agreed. "If we were in the middle of a mission that wasn't working out, we wouldn't quit. I don't think Vlore will, either."

"Great," McCarter snorted as he lit a Players cigarette. "Since you're so good at reading between the lines like you had a bloody ouija board, maybe you can tell us where to find Vlore while you're at it."

"He won't be in Belgrade," Katz stated. "Too risky. He knows Krrabe and the others can give us a detailed description of him. The man's an expert in disguise, but that also means he knows no disguise is foolproof. He'll head outside the city."

"Kosovo?" Mazuranic suggested. "Thousands of Albanian nationals are there. He might try to blend in among them."

"Maybe," Encizo said. "But most Albanians living in Yugoslavia aren't sympathetic to efforts to make Kosovo part of Albania. Vlore might figure it would be too dangerous to stay there. On the other hand, Kosovo is close to the border and he might want to be as near as possible if he has to flee to Albania in a hurry."

"Vlore speaks fluent Serbian," Katz reminded the others. "He doesn't have to blend in with Albanians. Most of the men under his command probably speak Serbian or Croatian as well."

"Well, we've got a country the size of the state of Wyoming to hunt for him," James said. "That's a lot of territory for a man to hide in. A lot for us to try to cover."

"And most of Yugoslavia consists of forests and mountains," Manning said thoughtfully. "Wouldn't it be logical to hide in the forests? Vlore has been trained in wilderness survival. The climate is good and he could conceal an army in the wooded mountain regions. If I were on the run back in the States, I'd be inclined to head for the forests of Canada or possibly Montana or Wyoming. I'd go where there were fewer people and more space to hide in."

"Vlore has spent enough time here to know the forests well," Katz added. "It's very possible you're right, but finding Vlore isn't going to be any easier if that's what he's done. For one thing, we have no idea what part of the country he may have fled to. There are forests and mountains in almost every republic and province of Yugoslavia.''

"So instead of looking for him, let's get him to come to us,'' Manning suggested. "We need a lure. A very attractive target that Vlore won't be able to resist. Something that would appear to offer him hope of being able to salvage his mission after all.''

"Any idea what that might be?'' Encizo asked.

"Not right off the top of my head,'' Manning admitted. "But we ought to be able to come up with something.''

"Well, let's try to make it as quickly as possible,'' Katz advised. "We don't have much time left. The KGB has an idea who we are and I wouldn't count on them honoring their truce for more than a few days. If the Russians decide we aren't going to find Vlore or that Vlore must be back in Albania, they'll probably declare open season on us.''

"We'll come up with something,'' Manning repeated. But he was not as sure of that as he tried to sound.

14

"I suspected you gentlemen were all insane when we first met in Rome two years ago," Major Mario Bianco said as he stepped into the limousine bus at the Belgrade Airport Terminal. "Now I'm certain of it."

"Thanks for coming, Major," Gary Manning replied with a grin. "And congratulations on your promotion. You were still a captain when we met before."

The tall lean Italian officer had good reason to remember the men of Phoenix Force—although he had never known them by that title or by their real names. A gang of international terrorists had seized control of the Vatican and the President of the United States had sent a special elite team of commandos to assist the Italian authorities in dealing with the crisis. Bianco had been somewhat miffed by this at the time. After all, he was an officer of the carabinieri Parachute Battalion, which had been created to handle terrorist activity. Why bring in foreigners from America?

He soon learned the answer. Phoenix Force was the best fighting unit of its kind in the world. Six men had climbed over a wall to the Vatican and took on a small army of terrorists. Six men had handled the nightmare situation with a minimum of bloodshed. There had been little damage to the priceless treasures and property of the Vatican. Phoenix Force imposed stricter security than the carabinieri could have hoped.

Bianco, promoted to field grade rank after the episode, received a great deal of recognition and praise for his role in freeing the Vatican. Yet he knew the commandos of Phoenix Force had really saved the hostage holy city. Bianco had wondered about them many times since that day. He wondered if they were still alive, and sometimes, when he heard stories about heroic actions by a small elite team in foreign lands, he wondered if these were reports of missions conducted by the same men who had rescued the Vatican.

"This is Colonel Mazuranic of the Federal Security Committee," Katz said, introducing Bianco to the Yugoslavian intel officer as the limousine bus left the terminal. "He's working with us. You've no doubt heard about the trouble in Belgrade recently?"

"Yes," Bianco said with a nod. "But I thought they'd arrested the terrorists responsible following a gun battle just yesterday. I know of no other details, except that everybody seemed convinced the terrorists were responsible for the shootings."

"They aren't terrorists in the normal sense of the term," Katz explained, aware that because of the news blackout, Bianco would know very little except what he had been told. "They're Albanian espionage agents and it isn't over yet. That's why we asked the Italian government to send you as commander of a squad of personally chosen carabinieri troops."

"I'm flattered you have such faith in me," Bianco replied. "But I'm very puzzled by your request for men who are not only skilled commandos but familiar with movie cameras, carpentry, horseback riding, stage lighting and other rather strange skills for this sort of mission. Then I was told we'd be working with that American film director Arthur Osland and that muscle-bound German actor Hans Schwartz—"

"Hans Schlange, and he was originally from Austria," Manning corrected him. "I think he recently became a naturalized U.S. citizen. His last two films made a lot of money at the box office. Don't be too critical of either Osland or Schlange. They know they're putting their lives in danger, but they agreed to come to Yugoslavia anyway."

"And my carabinieri soldiers are supposed to pretend to be part of Osland's film crew while he's making some idiotic gladiator movie with the muscle man?" Bianco asked. "That is what you have in mind, isn't it?"

"That's right," Katz confirmed.

"I was right," the Italian officer said shaking his head. "You are insane."

"I realize this is all very irregular, Major," Mazuranic began. "You see, the American movie director had planned to make the film here in Yugoslavia before the embassy incident. When the trouble occurred, Osland was encouraged to film in Italy instead.''

"The people who were financing insisted he shoot in Italy," Manning added. "Well, now the movie is going to be funded by a richer source. The United States government is paying for it—indirectly, of course. In return for this, Osland has agreed to film in Yugoslavia and help us with the cover we need for bait to draw the remaining Albanian agents from hiding.''

"You people arranged all this in less than two days?" Bianco glared at Manning and Katz as if they'd just announced they could walk on water and bring the dead back to life. "And this was all just to sneak the carabinieri into Yugoslavia?''

"That's part of it," Katz answered. "Naturally, Osland hired Italian personnel to work on the movie. It is reasonable to assume he'd bring part of the Italian crew with him to Yugoslavia. This is a good cover for your people entering the country.''

"Since the Albanians obviously have a number of sleeper agents planted here," Mazuranic added, "we needed to get reliable people from outside Yugoslavia. Mr. Gray and Mr. Green here mentioned that they'd worked with you and the carabinieri before. Time, distance and Osland's film locale made you the logical choice under the circumstances.''

"Is Yugoslavia going to return this favor by returning the ownership of the south Trieste area to Italy?" Bianco asked dryly.

The province of Trieste is located in northeast Italy. During the Second World War, the Yugoslavians seized the capital city of Trieste, a valuable port. Italy and Yugoslavia argued about the possession of Trieste for thirty years. Finally, in 1975, the two countries signed a treaty acknowledging south Trieste as belonging to Yugoslavia. Obviously, not all Italians were satisfied with this decision.

"Don't be a pain in the ass, Major," Manning told Bianco. "This doesn't have anything to do with Trieste. It won't help Italy if Yugoslavia is torn apart by internal violence and cut off from the rest of the world."

"Or if the Albanians win their ultimate goal, and take over south Trieste with the rest of Yugoslavia," Katz added. "Trieste is a free port under the Yugoslavians. Do you think an isolationist country like Albania would continue that policy?"

"That couldn't happen," Bianco said with a shrug. "Albania is too small and underdeveloped to take over Yugoslavia."

"Probably right," Katz agreed. "But if they succeed to a degree and cause enough internal unrest, the Soviets will roll across the Bulgarian border and move in. There's a real danger this could happen. Do you like the idea of having a Soviet satellite nation for a neighbor?''

"All right," Bianco said with a sigh. "I apologize for even mentioning Trieste, Colonel Mazuranic. Of course, I'm eager to help you protect your country from these Albanian agents and I agree this danger to Yugoslavia is a threat to the peace and well-being of Europe, if not the entire world."

"I'm so glad," the Yugoslavian officer said dryly.

"But I still don't understand how the movie crew is going to draw out the enemy," Bianco commented.

"Well, it's the best plan we could come up with," Manning said a bit sheepishly.

"It has about a fifty-fifty chance of working," Katz explained. "All things considered, the odds aren't bad."

"I know what you fellows regard as fair odds," Bianco said, recalling the Vatican incident. "Where are the other members of your team? They are still working with you, yes?"

"You're wondering if any of them have been killed since we met you in Rome, right?" Manning asked, guessing the reason for Bianco's awkwardness. "They're all still alive and you'll see them all soon. One guy who was with us in Rome isn't here, but he does this sort of thing only as a sideline."

Manning referred to John Trent, a Japanese-American who operated a martial arts school in San Francisco. Trent was also a highly trained *ninja* warrior. Although he had assisted Phoenix Force on four missions, Trent was not a regular member of the team.

"A sideline?" Bianco raised his eyebrows.

"Everybody needs a hobby," Manning said with a shrug. "Anyway, our three partners are still at the airport to meet Osland and his film crew and to make sure the director understands what we expect of him while he's in Yugoslavia. Since Osland, Schlange and some of the others are civilians, we'll do our best to minimize the danger to them during this mission. Still, there's no way we can guarantee anybody's safety."

"You are aware this could all turn into a terrible disaster?" Bianco inquired, his tone expressing serious doubts about what he had heard about their plan thus far.

"Yes, we're aware of that," Katz answered. "We'll just have to try to prevent that from happening."

"I hope so," Bianco replied, wondering if he should have stayed in Italy.

ARTHUR OSLAND AND HANS SCHLANGE were met at the lobby of the Beograd Intercontinental Hotel by an array of newspaper, television and radio reporters. The press consisted of an international mix of Europeans and Americans, and even a team of reporters from Japan. Viktor Pasternak and the Moscow press did not attend. The Soviets didn't regard American films shot in Yugoslavia as vital news.

A pear-shaped, middle-aged man who liked to wear flowery Hawaiian shirts and baseball caps, Osland looked more like a caricature of an American tourist than a movie director. Cameras flashed and microphones hovered near Osland's face. Schlange stood behind his director, towering above him. Six and a half feet tall, the Austrian-born was an Olympic athlete, a gold medal winner for weight lifting. A ruggedly good-looking man with a powerful muscular body and an amiable personality, Schlange had a natural screen presence that led to movie offers after the Olympics. Schlange's film roles were action movies that included lots of scenes that displayed his awesome physique.

"On behalf of everybody involved in *The Viking Warlord*," Osland began, addressing the microphones and TV cameras, "I want to say we're very pleased to be here in Yugoslavia. As you know, this is where we had originally planned to film *The Viking Warlord* until the terrorist activity occurred. A lot of my backers didn't want me to come here even now, but I say Yugoslavia has taken care of that problem and it's time for us all to go back to living our lives and doing our jobs as before. If we let these lousy terrorists worry us, if they can scare us away from our goals in life, then they win. That's not gonna happen."

"So you see the making of this movie as a political statement?" a French journalist asked.

"You mean the movie?" Osland asked with a grin. "Hell no. *The Viking Warlord* is just rousing entertainment. Sex and violence. I like my movies to make a profit in the box office."

"No, no," the journalist said awkwardly. "I mean your coming here to Yugoslavia so soon after the embassy shooting and other incidents. Is this a gesture of friendship between the United States and Yugoslavia?"

"You might say that," Osland answered. "I mean it's just an action film. No Academy Award material and I don't think they'll have me up for a Nobel Prize either. Still, industries throughout the world have to be able to deal with each other. That includes the motion picture industry. I think it's important that Americans and our friends in West Europe such as the Italians—of which we have several among our crew—realize it's safe to come to Yugoslavia now. All the talk about severing relations with the U.S. is over now. Everything appears to be going back to normal. That includes shooting movies in Yugoslavia because it doesn't cost much to film here."

"Mr. Schlange?" a BBC reporter began. "Do you share Mr. Osland's feelings or do you have some misgivings about filming here after the events that occurred so recently in Belgrade and the Kosovo district?"

"No, I do not worry of this," Schlange answered in thickly accented English. "We are going to make a movie because the terrorists, they are finished. They have lost and Yugoslavia is still friends with United States. I am an American citizen now. I want America to keep all its friends in other countries and making this movie is one way to show we still get along okay."

"What sort of character do you play in the movie, Hans?" an American reporter asked.

"I am Viking warlord," Schlange replied with a broad grin. "Star of the show. I get to kill a lot of people with a big plastic sword. Fondle naked women and lie in bed with them. Is hard work, but someone has to do it, I guess."

The reporters chuckled at Schlange's remark. Yakov Katzenelenbogen and Gary Manning sat at the back of the room, watching the press conference. Calvin James and Rafael Encizo were among the reporters, watching for any sign of suspicious behavior by the news hounds. It was unlikely Argon Vlore's people would try anything at the Beograd Intercontinental, but Phoenix Force was not dismissing any possibilities.

"Well," Katz remarked as he tapped the ash from a cigarette into a shell-shaped brass ashtray, "there's our bait. Now we can only hope Vlore will go after it."

"I hope so," Manning replied. "This was my idea. Brognola wasn't too thrilled about it, either. He had to pull a lot of strings to arrange this. If Vlore doesn't go for the bait, Hal's gonna be really pissed with me."

"He won't be too happy with any of us," Katz said with a shrug. He glanced about the posh lobby of the deluxe hotel. Except for the press conference with the movie people, everything seemed normal. The hotel staff watched the visiting celebrities with fascination. "If we guessed wrong, Vlore has gone back to Albania anyway, and there's nothing to worry about."

"Or he might not go for the bait," Manning said with a frown. "Hell, if he's hiding out in a forest somewhere he may not even know about *The Viking Warlord*."

"This press conference is getting coverage in newspapers, and on television and radio," Katz reminded his Canadian partner. "Vlore will still have some form of communication with what's going on outside his hideout. He'll find out about it."

David McCarter and Colonel Mazuranic crossed the lobby. As usual, the Briton's sport coat and trousers looked as if he'd slept in them and tossed and turned all night. The popular image of the dapper English gentleman didn't apply to McCarter. Mazuranic, on the other hand, was neatly dressed in a light blue double-breasted suit with a white shirt and striped tie. They looked as if they were on their way to a rehearsal of a remake of *The Odd Couple*.

"The hotel security is pretty tight," McCarter announced as they joined Katz and Manning. "I guess the Beograd Intercontinental doesn't want a reputation for being a high-class hangout for burglars and riffraff. The regular hotel security personnel are quite a bit better than average. We were stopped a couple of times while we were checking the place out.''

"The police commissioner supplied us with some extra officers in plain clothes and they'll help cover the security here," Mazuranic added. "I doubt Vlore will try anything in Belgrade. Especially when he learns the film crew will be shooting on location in forest land in southern Serbia. Fewer witnesses, no police and plenty of natural camouflage and cover for their activities.''

"We're hoping we can lure Vlore to the forests for the same reasons," Katz stated. "Besides, there's less of a chance innocent bystanders will be harmed if we can fight the enemy outside the city.''

"Have these blokes been giving a convincing performance?" McCarter asked, tilting his head toward Osland and Schlange, who were still being interviewed by the international press corps.

"Yeah," Manning replied. "They've been emphasizing that they're confident the United States and Yugoslavia have mended all diplomatic fences and the terrorist threat is over. In short, they've been indirectly rubbing the Albanians' noses in the fact their scheme has fallen apart.''

"They didn't mention the Albanians by name, did they?" Mazuranic asked with concern in his tone. "My government is still trying to determine how to best handle the political ramifications of this situation. Both the United States and the Soviet Union have agreed to keep the Albanian connection secret until we decide how to best deal with the fact that a neighboring country has been trying to subvert us."

"No, they didn't mention Albania," Katz assured him. "They only referred to 'terrorists.' I hope your government realizes this can't be covered up much longer. Too many people know about it and with the governments of both the United States and the Soviet Union aware of the Albanian involvement, the situation is going to become a political stink within a few days. Both governments will probably claim they're doing Yugoslavia a favor by keeping this business confidential, but both are actually doing it for their own reasons."

"I fail to see what they have to gain from this," the Yugoslavian officer said with a frown.

"The American government is relieved to be pretty much off the hook right now," Manning supplied the answer. "But it may soon want something from Yugoslavia in return for its cooperation and to compensate for the U.S. embassy and the CIA being falsely accused in the beginning. Probably something like encouraging Yugoslavia to sever relations and trade with Albania and trying to urge other Western European countries to do likewise."

"There's a strong possibility we'll do that anyway," Mazuranic said with a shrug.

"First you have to find out if the Albanian government is responsible or if this was all a scheme Director Progen conjured up on his own," Katz stated. "Personally, I'd be delighted to see the present Albanian government fall apart, but not at the expense of your country. Albania would surely retaliate by carrying out more subversive actions against Yugoslavia. More violence. More bloodshed. Albania would lose in the end, but it would cost your country dearly. Eventually, the present form of government in Albania is going to fold up anyway. Let it die a natural death from within and the people will be inclined to form a new government probably similar to that of their successful neighbors in Yugoslavia."

"The Americans might just want your country to agree to setting up more listening posts along the Bulgarian border," McCarter added. "Just as the Soviets might want such posts along the borders of Italy, Greece, Austria or even Hungary. Lots of creeping capitalism in Hungary, you know. Soviets are probably a bit worried about that."

"The Soviets will probably want more than listening posts," Katz stated. "Actually, Moscow may have agreed to maintain silence about the Albanians because it's hoping the situation here will get worse. Then it can condemn both Yugoslavia and Albania as examples of what happens to Communist nations that fail to follow Soviet doctrine. Since there are already pro-Soviet groups, especially among the militant Croatians, the KGB can start stirring up more trouble by encouraging and supporting these groups. Yugoslavia will be a lot better off if you can wrap this up without getting any more involvement with either the West or East."

"Amazing," Mazuranic said with a smile. "You fellows were sent by the American government, yet you're warning me about possible problems with the Americans."

"We're not warning you about America," Katz corrected. "We're simply saying Washington might decide to take advantage of Yugoslavia's plight to do something politicians and military strategists might consider to be to their favor. Yet the best interests of the United States will actually be served by letting Yugoslavia continue as it has been for the past thirty years."

"Yugoslavia is a Communist country, but you're independent of the Soviets and not part of the Warsaw Pact," Manning stated. "Your people have more rights and privileges than most people in other Communist countries and even some countries that are *supposed* to be democracies. I can't say I care too much for the one-party socialist system of government or the amount of government control Yugoslavia still has of many businesses and of the media, but you've still got more freedom here than any of the Iron Curtain countries. You've also got a growing level of free enterprise in Yugoslavia."

"Creeping capitalism again," Mazuranic remarked.

"It's not a dirty word, mate," McCarter told him. "All the Communist countries are slowly getting it. Hungary, Czechoslovakia, even the Soviet Union to a degree."

"That's because the strict rules of socialism won't work in a modern economy," Katz added. "What really matters is that Yugoslavia has become a model of a Communist country getting along with the Western democracies. To be honest, Yugoslavia has become a blend of communism and capitalism and has been leaning more toward the latter. That's why Yugoslavia is doing pretty well on its own and why we don't want to see any drastic changes that might hurt the progress your country has already made."

"I heartily agree," Mazuranic replied. "But this may all be out of our hands if your plan doesn't work."

"Well," Manning said with a sigh. "Let's hope it works or a lot of people might be more than a little bit disappointed."

"Some will be more than a little bit dead," McCarter added in a grim matter-of-fact tone. "That's the sort of thing folks don't get over."

15

Hans Schlange drew a four-foot long replica of a medieval broadsword from a leather scabbard on his belt. The replica appeared to be made of polished bronze, yet the sword was really plastic. Fairly hard plastic, because it had to endure a lot of punishment. Four stuntmen, also armed with plastic swords, formed a semicircle in front of Schlange.

Schlange was dressed in his Viking warlord costume—baggy trousers, goatskin boots and a helmet with two great curved horns. He didn't wear a shirt and his bulging weight-lifter muscles were on display. A leather strap across his massive chest contained several daggers in sheaths. A short-handled battle-ax with a double-edged plastic blade was thrust in his belt.

Gary Manning watched Schlange work the sword in a series of fancy figure-eight strokes as the first stuntman approached. The Canadian noticed Schlange displayed some expertise with the plastic blade. The actor had obviously taken some kendo lessons. The stuntman attacked, Schlange blocked the guy's plastic blade with his own sword and delivered a diagonal cut to the man's chest. The stunt guy threw up his arms and opened his mouth in mock agony as he fell backward. Stage blood seeped from a small rubber bag under the man's sheepskin vest.

An audience of Yugoslavian spectators applauded and gasped as they watched Schlange dodge another stuntman's sword attack and strike his plastic weapon across the second opponent's back. The stuntman arched his spine dramatically and spit a mouthful of stage blood, staggered forward and tumbled to the ground. The remaining pair of stuntmen waited until Schlange turned and stepped on his mark for the right camera angle.

"Not a bad show, huh?" Arthur Osland asked when he noticed Manning watching the choreographed sword fight. "These guys have rehearsed this scene several times before. Hans likes to do his own stunts and he's a champion athlete, of course. The insurance won't allow him to do high-risk stuff, but we let him do most of his own stunts."

"That's great," Manning remarked without enthusiasm as he raised a pair of binoculars to his eyes. "But I still wish you hadn't agreed to let these spectators attend the first day of shooting. Too many innocent bystanders."

The Canadian scanned the surrounding trees and rock formations. Osland's crew had set up on location at a site in a forest region near the Morava River. More than two hundred civilians had come to watch some of the action scenes being filmed. Carpenters had even built bleachers for the spectators, to keep them from wandering about and possibly getting injured, or from straying into camera range. They would have to reshoot if somebody in modern clothes and carrying a pocket camera appeared in the background of some of *The Viking Warlord* footage.

"It wasn't my idea, fella," Osland told Manning. "Somebody in the Yugoslavian government wanted us to let sightseers attend the shooting. The American ambassador agreed. They seem to think it'd be good public relations for the United States and Yugoslavia. Helps to show everybody that the terrorism is really over. Wouldn't it be nice if they were right?"

"Yeah," Manning commented, still searching the trees with his binoculars. "But I wouldn't count on it being over."

The forest of poplar and ash trees seemed peaceful. Green treetops swayed gently amid the clear blue summer sky above. Yet the sky itself wasn't silent. A Lockheed commercial helicopter hovered overhead. David McCarter piloted the chopper while a pair of cameramen filmed the sword fight from the air. The British commando was also scanning the forests for evidence of enemy presence. The cameramen on board the aircraft were carabinieri paratroopers armed with assault rifles as well as motion picture cameras.

Rafael Encizo, Calvin James and Mihailo Krleza patroled the perimeter of the film site. Each rode in a Land Rover with a Belgrade police driver and scanned the area with binoculars. They all had walkie-talkies to contact the others if they saw anything out of the ordinary—not that any of them was quite certain what ordinary meant for a motion picture crew.

Yakov Katzenelenbogen and Colonel Mazuranic were stationed among the trailers and tents set up for the film crew. Stunt people, makeup artists, costume personnel in wardrobe, special effects experts, supporting cast members and others were clustered among the makeshift housing to watch Schlange's sword duel. Katz and the Yugoslavian intel officer were more interested in the surrounding area than the mock battle. The fight was fixed, anyway.

Schlange had dispatched his third stuntman opponent with a sword thrust. Osland called, "Cut," and the filming stopped. The director approached Schlange and the stuntmen. The audience applauded. Osland and Schlange bowed to the crowd. The two stuntmen who had already been "killed" sat up and waved at the spectators. A propman handed Schlange a sword identical to the one he used for the fight except that the blade was cut in half. The special effects expert brought a jar of stage blood to paint the sword and smear the chest of the stuntman who had just been "stabbed."

"Okay," Osland began, speaking through a megaphone. "Let's get camera two over here for a close-up. Tom, you got that sword tip set up yet?"

"Just a second, Art," the special effects man answered as he adjusted a foot-long plastic blade between the shoulder blades of the stunt guy who supposedly had been run through by Schlange's sword. "Still gotta put some blood on it."

"Okay, okay," Osland said, nodding his head. "Everything looks good so far. I think we can get everything in one take, guys. Sorry to push it, but we want to make the most of the sunlight."

"We're ready here, Art," the special effects man announced as he guided Schlange's half sword to a "bloody" spot on the stuntman's chest. Schlange nodded.

Haxhi Gheg and Adil Lezhe were among the spectators seated at the bleachers. The Albanian agents pretended to find the show fascinating and forced themselves to cheer and applaud with the others. A psychotic who enjoyed killing and considered the power to take human life to be a godlike talent, Gheg found the mock violence of the sword fight disgusting. The moviemakers knew nothing about death, yet they glorified it for the entertainment of the masses. Gheg found this offensive. Almost sacrilegious.

Gheg seemed to feel invulnerable among the Yugoslavian spectators. They were lesser mortals, sheep waiting to be slaughtered that failed to notice a wolf in their fold. Adil Lezhe didn't share his comrade's arrogant self-confidence. A sleeper agent who had been living in the Kosovo Province for two years, Lezhe had almost forgotten he was an Albanian secret agent until Argon Vlore had arrived to call him into active service. Lezhe was not ready for this. He had gotten soft and fat during his time as an agent in place. In truth, he did not wish to return to Albania and he did not have any desire to harm any Yugoslavians.

Lezhe, however, had even less desire to have his throat cut by Haxhi Gheg, and he had no doubt the swarthy knife artist would kill him if he failed to carry out his part of the mission. Lezhe had been trained in the use of explosives. The camera that hung from a strap around his neck contained nearly a kilo of an RDX plastic explosive. The detonator, blasting cap and timing device were in his camera bag, disguised as rolls of film and flash attachment.

The film crew shot some brief footage of Schlange running the stuntman through with the half sword. The victim trembled in mock agony with stage blood oozing from his lips. The shot ended. The director stopped filming to prepare the next part of the fight scene. This required the fourth stuntman to attack Schlange with a sword stroke. There was to be a close-up of Schlange's hand drawing the battle-ax from his belt as he blocked the opponent's blade with the sword in his other hand. Then Schlange would break the other man's sword with a blow from the battle-ax and chop the double-edged blade into the stuntman's neck.

This footage required several shots and the prop-man had to replace the stunt guy's sword with a weapon with a plastic blade that would break when Schlange hit it. Tom, the special effects man, also prepared another battle-ax with part of the blade carved out so it would appear to have chopped into the stuntman's neck for another colorful close-up. Naturally, this required more stage blood for the desired effect.

Gheg dug an elbow into Lezhe's ribs and tilted his head to one side. Both men rose and stepped down from the bleachers. They walked around the crowd and pretended to move toward the visitors' parking area, a clearing where numerous cars, bikes and mopeds were gathered. Gheg pulled down the zipper of his windbreaker and took a pack of cigarettes from his shirt pocket. He lit a cigarette and pretended to watch the crew prepare the last shots of the fight scene, but Gheg's eyes scanned the area like a hawk. His jacket remained open in case he needed to reach for either the Tokarev pistol or fighting dagger hidden under the cloth.

While Gheg stood guard between the bleachers and the improvised parking lot, Adil Lezhe crept to the rear of the bleachers and ducked under them. He glanced up at the elevated benches, legs and backsides of spectators seated above him. Lezhe's hands trembled as he took the camera from his neck and placed it on the ground. He was afraid someone would glance down and see him as he opened the camera bag and removed the detonator and blasting cap.

"¡*MADRE DE DIOS!*" Rafael Encizo rasped as he lowered his Bushnell binoculars. He grabbed his walkie-talkie. "Attention all ground stations," he spoke into the mouthpiece.

"Command central," Katz's voice replied. "Report. Over."

"I just spotted a man under the bleachers and it looks like he's put something under there," Encizo explained. "Could be a bomb. There's another guy hanging around nearby. I think they might be together."

"Keep them covered and don't let them get away," Katz instructed. "Patrol Three, move toward Two's position in case they need backup. Patrol One, stay in place and watch for enemy backup team. Fifty-fifty chance there's one out there. No shooting unless you have to and then use only pistols unless automatic fire is mandatory. Try to take at least one of them alive."

"On our way," Encizo replied as he switched off the radio.

"So the terrorists are here," Sergeant Mesa Preseren commented nervously. He was the Belgrade cop in charge of driving the Land Rover with Encizo.

"That's how it looks," the Cuban warrior confirmed as he opened his field jacket to make certain he could reach the 9 mm H&K pistol on his hip, the Walther PPK in shoulder leather and the Cold Steel Tanto in a belt sheath if necessary. "Drive to the parking area. They've probably got a car there."

"Da," Preseren replied. "Uh, yes, sir."

The sergeant shifted gears and the Land Rover bolted for the parking area. Encizo and Preseren arrived as Haxhi Gheg and Adil Lezhe walked to the parking section. Preseren parked the Land Rover behind a minibus that concealed the patrol vehicle from the Albanians' view. Encizo hopped from the Rover and drew his H&K PS-9 as he crept around the rear of the bus.

Gheg and Lezhe walked quickly, eager to reach a small blue Volkswagen Beetle. Encizo waited until Lezhe fished the keys out of a pocket before he stepped into the open with the pistol aimed at the two Albanians.

"Beograd policiju!" Preseren announced as he moved around the front of the bus with an M-57 pistol in both fists.

Haxhi Gheg whirled and reached inside his jacket for the Tokarev holstered under his arm. He froze when he saw Encizo's pistol pointed at his chest. The Cuban smiled and nodded as if inviting the Albanian to try to draw his piece. Gheg guessed he was facing an opponent who would not hesitate to squeeze the trigger if he accepted the challenge. He slowly raised his hands instead. Lezhe followed Gheg's example.

"Tell them to get spread-eagled, Mesa," Encizo told Preseren.

"Spread-eagled?" the police sergeant asked, confused.

"Tell them to put their hands on the roof of the car and spread their legs apart," Encizo explained. "Then we search 'em for weapons. Okay?"

"Right," Preseren replied. "I understand."

The cop snapped orders in rapid Serbo-Croatian. Gheg and Lezhe placed their hands on the roof of the VW and parted their legs. Preseren jogged forward and jammed the muzzle of his M-57 in the small of Gheg's back. Encizo stepped behind Lezhe and jabbed the barrel of his H&K at the base of the Albanian's skull.

"Camera bag first," he said, sliding the strap from Lezhe's shoulder. "Don't play dumb. Even if you don't understand English, you know what I mean."

Lezhe moved his arm and the camera bag slipped off to fall at his feet. Encizo quickly frisked the Albanian, checking for weapons at the small of his back and sleeves before binding the man's wrists together behind him with a set of plastic riot cuffs. Preseren patted down Gheg and soon found the killer's Tokarev pistol. He slid it from its holster and held it high for Encizo to see.

"Look at this," the police sergeant announced.

Gheg suddenly whirled and rammed an elbow under Preseren's jaw. The man groaned and fell on his back. The Tokarev slipped from his grasp when he hit the ground, but he held on to the unfired M-57. Gheg's boot kicked the pistol from the sergeant's hand and sent the gun skidding under a Yugo. Gheg's other boot delivered another kick between Preseren's legs. The police sergeant convulsed in agony and clutched his manhood, vomiting on the ground.

Encizo swung his pistol toward Gheg and ordered him to halt. Lezhe used his knees to push away from the car and rammed his shoulder into the Cuban's extended arm. The clumsy attack knocked the H&K autoloader from Encizo's fist.

"*¡Cristo!*" the Cuban snarled as he grabbed Lezhe's hair with one hand and rammed a knee under the Albanian's rib cage.

Lezhe doubled up with a gasp and Encizo pushed him like a battering ram at Gheg. The agile Albanian hit man sidestepped and Lezhe, gasping, fell beside the dazed Preseren. Gheg's hand streaked inside his jacket and reappeared holding a fighting dagger.

Gheg lunged at Encizo. The Cuban dodged the knife thrust and yanked his Cold Steel Tanto from leather. They were fighting at extreme close quarters, and Encizo realized he would not be able to draw the PPK before Gheg could slash or lunge with the dagger. The Tanto took a split second less time to draw.

The Albanian blademan saw the big steel weapon in his opponent's fist. The Tanto was a modern version of an ancient samurai fighting knife. Sunlight danced on the flawless cold steel blade. Gheg smiled and squared off with Encizo. He was confident of victory. Haxhi Gheg had never lost a knife fight. Most of his previous opponents were dead. He didn't know that Encizo's record as a successful knife fighter was even more impressive.

However, Encizo didn't share Gheg's confidence. All confrontations with lethal weapons are unpredictable and knife fights are no exception. Gheg held his dagger low, the blade partly shielded by his other hand. The Albanian crouched low, knees bent and feet balanced. No amateur with a knife, he was at least ten years younger than Encizo. Gheg was also wiry and built for speed. The Cuban no doubt had more experience, but youth and speed are great assets for a knife fighter.

Gheg thrust his knife, an unexpected move because a dagger is designed for stabbing more than for cutting. Narrowly avoiding the rapid lunge, Encizo slashed at his opponent's arm. It had already swung clear and Encizo's blade cut only air. The Albanian delivered a backhand stroke and his dagger sliced the fabric of Encizo's shirtfront. A sharp pain stung the Cuban's chest as skin split open from the cut.

Encizo had been cut before and he didn't back off. His Tanto responded with an upward slash. Gheg jumped back, but Encizo's blade caught the Albanian's left shoulder. The sharp cold steel edge sliced into skin and muscle. Gheg cried out with pain and slashed at Encizo's face.

The Cuban weaved away from the attack. Gheg's arm swung in a loop and lunged a knife thrust for Encizo's chest. The Cuban warrior avoided the blade and slashed at his opponent's wrist. The nimble Albanian swung his arm wide of the cut and with his left hand seized the Phoenix pro's wrist.

Gheg pinned down Encizo's knife hand and thrust his dagger at the commando's throat. The Cuban's shoulder dropped and he leaned away from the knife lunge. A burning pain under his jaw told Encizo he had not quite dodged the dagger entirely. The sharp blade had cut a shallow wound between neck and jawbone. With his left hand Encizo snared Gheg's wrist and pushed the dagger away.

Struggling, each man held the other's knife at bay. Encizo tried to knee Gheg in the groin but the Albanian blocked with a thigh. Gheg's head snapped forward and butted Encizo in the forehead. The Phoenix fighter's skull throbbed and lights burst in front of his eyes, but he held on.

Gheg forcibly swung his body to the right, trying to break free of Encizo's grip. The Cuban moved with his opponent and suddenly thrust both arms overhead. Gheg's arms rose with the Phoenix pro's, surprised by the muscular Cuban's upper body strength. Encizo bent his knees, turned his hips and twisted about. His opponent was also turned around and found himself back-to-back with Encizo.

The Cuban warrior dropped to one knee and bent forward. Gheg cried out as he tumbled backward over Encizo's crouched form. The Albanian crashed to the ground hard. Both men lost their grip on the other's wrist, but Encizo hopped to his feet first. The Cuban feinted a knife slash. Gheg swung a wild dagger stroke in response, although Encizo's weapon did not come close to the Albanian. Instead, Gheg left himself vulnerable to another attack from a different direction.

Encizo kicked Gheg's face. The Albanian's head snapped back from the impact of Encizo's boot heel against his cheekbone. He groaned and sprawled sideways to the ground. Encizo stepped forward. He planned to stomp on Gheg's wrist and force him to give up the dagger. The Albanian's legs suddenly shot out in a scissors kick and snared Encizo's shins and calves. An adroit twist threw the Cuban off balance.

The Phoenix commando landed hard on his back, the wind driven from his lungs. Encizo mentally cursed himself for being careless. He had been so certain he'd vanquished Gheg that he had walked right into a trap. Instead of stepping forward to disarm the Albanian, he should have stepped back and drawn his Walther PPK when he had the chance. Now he was flat on his back and Gheg was descending upon him with the dagger aimed at his heart.

Encizo saw the Albanian's furious bloodied face inches from his own. Gheg's eyes were filled with raw hatred, with the burning desire to destroy his opponent. Encizo saw the madness in Gheg's expression even as he pushed with his heels and left palm to move away from the dagger thrust. The Albanian's blade just touched Encizo's ribs, but sank deep into the ground.

The Cuban drove his Tanto upward and buried the six-inch steel blade in his opponent's solar plexus. The powerful thrust killed Haxhi Gheg. His mouth fell open, his eyes widened as though with disbelief that he was dead. His body twitched slightly and tumbled to the ground, Encizo's Tanto still jammed deeply into him.

"Oh, Jesus," Gary Manning gasped as he approached. The Cuban was covered with blood, most of which belonged to Gheg. "Don't move! I'll get a medic."

"I'm okay," Encizo assured him, slowly getting to his feet. "The bastard cut me a couple times, but he didn't cut me good enough. Where's the other one?"

"I pulled him to the ground," Preseren said sheepishly, one hand still massaging his genitals. "I hit him with my fist to keep him down. Sorry I was not much help...."

"It worked out okay," Encizo said as he noticed the other Albanian agent, Adil Lezhe, on his knees next to Inspector Mihailo Krleza. The Belgrade policeman had a pistol braced against the side of the Albanian's head. "What about the bomb?"

"You mean this?" Manning asked, holding Lezhe's camera by its neck strap. "I found it and deactivated it. Loaded up with plastic explosives. Enough to blow up just about everybody seated in the bleachers."

"That would have been a real bang-up ending to Osland's little performance," Encizo mused. He winced as he touched the cut at his neck. His fingers, he noticed, were stained with crimson. "Well, your idea worked. They took the bait. What's our next move?"

"That'll depend on what information we can squeeze out of this guy," Manning answered, tilting his head toward Lezhe.

16

Phoenix Force and its allies combed the area in search of a backup team, but apparently Gheg and Lezhe had been on their own or, more likely, the backup team had observed the fate of its comrades and fled. Argon Vlore was too professional not to have an observation team of some sort set up in order to report on the success or failure of the two would-be saboteurs. Probably personnel miles away from the site with telescopes.

This meant Vlore would surely know his plan had failed. He would probably assume one or both agents had been taken alive. Vlore would also assume his present hiding place would be in jeopardy, and he would certainly strike camp and move to a new locale. Vlore probably had a new site already chosen for such an emergency—a bit of information he would not share with a couple of guys he sent on a mission to blow up a bunch of civilians.

Once again, Phoenix Force was faced with two enemies: its flesh and blood opponents, and time. Fortunately, the film crew had finished shooting for the day and the visitors had departed in their vehicles.

A couple of civilians did notice some patches of crimson on the ground at the parking area. These looked like blood and the people who examined it were quite sure that it was. Stage blood, naturally. The special effects expert must have spilled some when he first arrived. Not surprising, because they certainly used a lot of stage blood for the movie.

Adil Lezhe was smuggled into a trailer used by Phoenix Force and Colonel Mazuranic as a temporary field headquarters. Calvin James was called in from Patrol One to help Katz and Mazuranic interrogate the prisoner. James's expertise in medicine and chemistry had led to an adept use of scopolamine since he joined Phoenix Force. The only reliable truth serum, scopolamine is also a very powerful drug and can be lethal if misused. James had never lost a subject due to the administration of this truth serum.

But that record might not stay intact. James examined Lezhe to determine the Albanian's physical condition before he prepared a scopolamine injection for the captive. A subject's age, weight, heartbeat, blood pressure, irregular breathing patterns caused by stress, and other information determined how much of the drug should be used or even if scopolamine could be used without running the risk of killing the subject.

"This dude is in pretty lousy shape," James explained. "His blood pressure is very high, he's nearly wheezing and I detected an irregular pattern to his heartbeat, which might be a heart murmur."

"You think he can survive the scopolamine if you use a smaller dose?" Katz asked.

"I wouldn't bet on it," James replied. "If the dose is too small the drug won't work. If it's too strong it'll kill him."

"That's a risk we have to take," Mazuranic stated.

"*We* have to take?" the black hardcase glared at him. "This guy's the one who might have his heart burst like a bubble and I'm the one who has to give him the drug. The idea of murdering that poor bastard doesn't appeal to me, man. I got a silly little aversion to killing a helpless man. One of those things that might make it kind of hard for me to live with myself in the future."

"That 'poor bastard' tried to kill two hundred Yugoslavian citizens today," the colonel said sharply. "I say that cancels out any regard we need to show for his well-being."

"Nothing will be gained by killing him," Yakov Katzenelenbogen commented thoughtfully. "Let's try to reason with this fellow. Will you translate for us, Colonel?"

"Very well," Mazuranic agreed with a sigh.

They turned to face Adil Lezhe. The Albanian sat on a cot, stripped to his underwear, hands cuffed behind his back and ankles strapped together. His soft, flabby body seemed pale and helpless. His round face was bruised, one eye swollen shut. Lezhe trembled and he breathed rapidly as the Phoenix Force commander and Colonel Mazuranic pulled up two folding chairs and sat across from him.

"All right," Katz began, tapping a Camel cigarette against a steel hook of his prosthetic arm. "Explain our situation to the prisoner. Tell him we know Vlore sent him and it's just a matter of time before we catch up with his boss. Time is something we don't have a lot of, however, and we want him to tell us where we can find Vlore."

Mazuranic translated the message into Serbo-Croatian. Lezhe did not reply. Katz lighted his cigarette before he continued.

"Tell him about the truth serum," Katz instructed. "Tell him that's why my partner gave him that medical examination. If we use the drug it will probably kill him. If he survives he'll still face charges of terrorism, two hundred counts of attempted murder and other crimes, which will mean that he'll spend the rest of his life in prison. However, we're prepared to offer him an alternative. Ask him if he'd like to live and not go to prison?"

Mazuranic continued to translate. Lezhe nodded eagerly when he heard the last question.

"That's what I thought," Katz remarked. He offered Lezhe a cigarette. The Albanian gratefully accepted it and Katz lit the Camel for the prisoner. "Here's the deal. Tell him if he cooperates with us he'll get a new identity and a new home outside Yugoslavia. This will include cosmetic surgery, language courses if necessary and a nest egg of money to start his new life. It's a one-time-only offer and it is as good a deal as he's going to get.''

Lezhe listened to Mazuranic explain the offer. He asked the Yugoslavian a question.

''He wants to know how he can be sure he can trust us to keep our word,'' Mazuranic told Katz.

''I can't really show you proof that we'll keep our word,'' the Israeli admitted. ''But you know what will happen if you don't cooperate. If we were not honorable men we'd simply use torture to try to get you to talk. Perhaps you'd resist or perhaps you'd die from the experience. Still, we could crush your thumbs, cut off your nose or extract some teeth with a pair of pliers. Such injuries wouldn't be fatal and we could always do worse things if those didn't work.''

Lezhe trembled when Mazuranic translated once more. Katz smiled as he took the cigarette from Lezhe's lips and tapped off the ash.

''Tell him he won't be harmed if he helps us,'' Katz instructed. ''Otherwise, we'll use the scopolamine and take the chance it may kill him. Even if he survives he loses. Also, warn him if he lies to us we'll find out before we take him to Belgrade. That will mean we'll simply use the scopolamine later instead of sooner. The only way he wins is if he cooperates with us now. The choice is really quite simple. Death or imprisonment or a new life in Greece or Italy or wherever. That may not be a chance at Utopia, but it's the best he'll get.''

Mazuranic told Lezhe the deal. The Albanian took a deep breath and spoke to the colonel. Mazuranic turned to Katz and smiled.

"He said he needs a detailed map of the area," the Yugoslavian officer declared.

TWILIGHT HAD FALLEN as Phoenix Force and its allies headed for the site mapped out by Lezhe. Colonel Ivo Mazuranic reluctantly remained near the movie set with a group of Security Committee agents, Belgrade cops and a few Italian paratroopers in case the enemy decided to launch another attack there. Rafael Encizo was even less happy about being ordered to remain behind. However, Calvin James insisted that the wounds Encizo had received in the knife fight might reopen in a combat situation. The Cuban veteran realized he would put more lives than his own in jeopardy if he went into a crisis confrontation in less than peak condition. Encizo could do little but wish the others good luck and help Mazuranic prepare the defenses at the movie site.

Three vehicles traveled through the Serbian forest as dusk slowly descended. Gary Manning rode a Land Rover at the lead of the small caravan. The Yugoslavian who drove the vehicle was a heavy-set man with a shaggy red beard, named Vuk Andric. An ex-police officer in Budva, Andric had been kicked off the force after being arrested for poaching in the southern Serbian region. Andric was literally freed from his jail cell by Colonel Mazuranic after the poacher agreed to help in the mission in return for a full amnesty for his previous crimes.

Andric knew the local forests better than just about anyone they could have enlisted on such short notice. His training as a police officer, and before that as a soldier in the Yugoslavian Ground Forces, gave him some background in the procedures and weapons needed for the operation. Ironically, he had acquired his most valuable skills and knowledge through the illegal activities that had landed him in jail in the first place.

Yakov Katz and Major Mario Bianco followed in a deuce-and-a-half truck behind the Land Rover. Katz sat up front with Sergeant Mesa Preseren, who was once again working as a driver. Bianco was in the back with half a dozen of his carabinieri paratroopers. Calvin James and Inspector Mihailo Krleza sat in the front of another truck that brought up the rear of the column. The last vehicle also contained six Yugoslavians, three Belgrade policemen and three Security Committee agents. All were either former paratroopers or experienced in antiterrorism during operations in Croatia or Kosovo.

Above the caravan, the Lockheed helicopter cut through the sky, piloted by David McCarter, accompanied by two carabinieri troopers. The Briton used an infrared night-search light to see through the darkness. Like the other members in charge of vehicles below, McCarter wore a pair of light-density goggles to avoid the need for outside lights in the gloom. The chopper moved in a wide pattern because the sound of the big rotor blade would carry further than the rumble of the engines. If the enemy spotted the copter, McCarter didn't want to give away the approximate position of the ground vehicles as well. Besides, a chopper moving to and fro in the sky made a more difficult target than one moving in a straight line.

"If that Albanian turd is telling the truth, I think I have a fair notion where the enemy is camped," Vuk Andric told Manning for the third time since the trip began. "They'll be covered by treetops from the air and by rock walls from ground searches. That's where I'd hide if I was in Vlore's boots."

"Ja, mein Herr," Gary Manning replied wearily. Vuk did not speak English and Manning was unfamiliar with the Yugoslavian's language. They found a common language in German.

"In fact, *I* should have hidden in this area myself." Andric chuckled. "Maybe then I never would have been arrested for poaching. One learns from life, I suppose."

"Hopefully," the Canadian replied as he scanned the forest of ash and walnut trees with a pair of night-vision binoculars. "I don't like this setup. Too much cover. Even with night-vision gear we might not see them before they hear us."

"We're barely creeping across the forest," Andric told him. "Tires on grass. Engines hardly humming under their bonnets. I think you Americans worry too much."

"That's no great comfort coming from a man who was caught poaching in these very woods," Manning replied dryly. He saw something move among the trees. "Stop this thing. There's something up ahead."

"Probably a deer..." Vuk said with a shrug.

Suddenly, a large figure appeared from behind a tree trunk. A familiar tube-shaped object was braced across the man's shoulder. Manning recognized the weapon immediately as a Soviet RPG rocket launcher. The Canadian combat veteran grabbed his FAL assault rifle and jumped from the Land Rover. Hitting the ground, he bent his knees and executed a shoulder roll. Manning's left leg struck a tree trunk. He grunted from the pain and slithered around the base of the tree.

The violent rush of air being split by a large projectile ripped the quiet of the night. The RPG rocket streaked from the launcher and hit the Land Rover dead center. The vehicle exploded with a monstrous roar. Metal, glass and flaming gasoline spewed from the core of the explosion. Burning chunks of flesh and bone were all that remained of Vuk Andric.

Katz had seen Manning bail out of the Land Rover and shouted, "Get down!" The Israeli ducked under the dashboard of the cab of the deuce-and-a-half. Sergeant Mesa Preseren did not react fast enough. The exploding Land Rover drove metal shrapnel into the windshield of the truck. Glass exploded and shards were driven inside the cab with bulletlike force.

Preseren's body convulsed behind the wheel. Slivers of glass and metal had ripped his face into bloodied shreds. Both eyeballs were punctured, his throat was cut open and a daggerlike piece of steel shrapnel pierced his forehead. The sergeant's corpse slumped against the steering wheel as the truck continued to creep forward.

"It's an ambush!" Calvin James shouted as he opened the cab to the other truck and jumped out, M-16 held ready.

Inspector Mihailo Krleza followed his example. Major Bianco and his carabinieri troops emerged from the back of the first truck, weapons in hand. Automatic fire erupted from the trees. Two of the Italian paratroopers screamed and tumbled to the ground, their bodies pouring blood from a dozen bullet wounds.

Phoenix Force and its allies had assumed Argon Vlore would have been busy preparing to flee. The Albanian master spy probably would have if he had more time. Instead, Argon had spotted the caravan—probably with night-vision telescopes—and decided to meet the assault force with an offensive strike of his own. The Phoenix unit had rolled right into an ambush.

A dozen automatic rifles fired at the members of the Phoenix Force group to pin them down while the Albanian with the rocket launcher loaded his RPG and prepared to fire another projectile at the remaining vehicles. Katz forced open the door to the truck cab as the deuce-and-a-half slowly rolled toward the flaming wreckage of the Land Rover. Katz dived from the rig, Uzi in his left fist. The Israeli rolled to the cover of a tree as enemy projectiles ripped up chunks of dirt near his hurtling form.

James and most of the Italian and Yugoslavian forces either ducked behind the remaining truck or dashed for nearby tree trunks. Some of the carabinieri had dropped to the ground and adopted prone positions to fire their automatic rifles at the ambushers.

Bullets splintered tree bark and one Albanian fell backward with a 7.62 mm round through the forehead. Another dropped his weapon and slumped next to the trunk he used for cover. He placed a hand to the bullet wound in his shattered shoulder and quietly passed out.

However, most of the Albanian forces were untouched by the return fire. They responded with another murderous salvo of full-auto fury. The earth near the prone carabinieri riflemen erupted in a series of geysers of dirt torn up by enemy bullets. One Italian marksman sprawled lifeless on the ground, his skull split open by a rifle slug. Another rolled to the cover of a tree trunk while a third attempted to do likewise, but moved directly into a 3-round burst of enemy bullets.

The Albanian rocket man stepped forward with his RPG and fired the projectile into the advancing truck. At the same moment, Gary Manning spotted the guy and nailed the rocket man with a trio of FAL rifle rounds. The Albanian collapsed with his heart and lungs chopped to pieces. The truck exploded an instant later.

Manning retreated behind the cover of a tree trunk, but a flying section of the truck's door slammed into the Canadian's rifle and ripped the FAL from his grasp. Manning ducked low and covered his head as more debris fell. Flaming gasoline splashed the ground and the base of the tree Manning used for cover. There was no time to retrieve his rifle. Manning had to move behind another tree trunk or risk being roasted alive.

The RPG explosion destroyed the truck, but except for the corpse of the unfortunate Sergeant Preseren, the vehicle had been unoccupied. Calvin James raised his M-16 and slipped his finger into the trigger guard of the M-203 grenade launcher attached to the underside of the barrel. He leaned around the edge of the second truck and fired the launcher. A 40 mm grenade shell tore through the air into the enemy position.

The explosion sent two mangled Albanian corpses hurtling into view. Screams mingled with the echo of the blast and suggested other opponents had also been injured by James's grenade. He turned to Major Bianco.

Covered with sweat, the Italian officer gripped his Beretta AR-70 assault rifle so hard his knuckles appeared ready to burst from the skin.

"Get the men away from this truck," James ordered, taking another M-203 round from a pouch on his left hip. He started to load the grenade cartridge into the breech of his launcher. "They're blowin' the shit outta these vehicles and they'll do the same to anybody near 'em at the time."

"Yes," Bianco said, nodding his head in agreement.

Inspector Krleza had heard James's remark and began ordering the Yugoslavian troops to seek cover behind trees and rock formations. Another volley of enemy fire erupted. One Yugoslavian fighter collapsed with a line of bullet holes stitched across his back. Another doubled up and fell to the ground, both arms clutching his punctured abdomen.

Twin salvos of automatic fire streaked down from the sky to rake the Albanians' position. The two Italian commandos on board the Lockheed fired down at the enemy as David McCarter piloted the helicopter over the trees and rocks used by Vlore's men for cover. The British ace grunted with satisfaction when he saw several enemy bodies drop to the ground from the aerial attack.

"Grenades!" McCarter shouted to the carabinieri pair as the chopper moved directly above the enemy position.

The two Italians pulled the pins from fragmentation grenades and dropped the minibombs from the helicopter. They managed to toss six grenades before McCarter swung the Lockheed away from the Albanians' stronghold. The explosions below signaled the success of this tactic. Bursts of brilliant light erupted under the tops of trees. Two trunks snapped from the explosions and trees toppled within the forest below.

"That's the way, mates!" McCarter called back to his companions. "Blow the bleeding arses off those dirty buggers!"

The Lockheed turned around and the Italian gunners fired into the enemy position once more. Bodies twisted and convulsed from the impact of Beretta slugs. Yet other Albanian gunmen returned fire with an assortment of weapons. A bullet smashed a hole in the chopper's windscreen. A spiderweb pattern appeared in front of McCarter, but the bullet had lodged in the glass without penetrating. The Briton sucked in a tense breath and released a sigh of relief.

Other bullets raked the carriage of the chopper. One of the carabinieri soldiers gasped and dropped his AR-70. The rifle tumbled out the open sliding door and plunged to the ground below. The paratrooper clung to his support harness and swayed inside the chopper. He managed to slide the door shut with his left hand. His right arm had been broken by a slug to the elbow. He had also received another bullet wound in the right rib cage.

"Enrico has been hit!" the other Italian cried out.

"Do what you can for him!" McCarter replied as he swerved the chopper away from the battle zone. "We're pulling out!"

A large projectile streaked from the trees below. A long cometlike tail followed the missile as it headed straight for the Lockheed craft. McCarter glimpsed the RPG round in the sky and worked the cyclic control sticks and the rudder pedals. He grabbed the collective and lowered the copter a split second before the rocket reached its target.

The projectile hit the rotor blade. The chopper spun from the impact and plunged out of control. McCarter saw the ground rush up at the craft as he struggled with the controls. The crippled rotor blade failed to respond. The RPG round had failed to explode on impact and sailed somewhere into the forest beyond before it detonated. The explosion was barely noticed by McCarter. His ears were filled with the wild hum of the spinning copter, the choking groan of the engines and the hammerlike throbbing of his own heartbeat.

The chopper descended rapidly. McCarter forced the collective up to try to slow the descent. He worked the cyclic, but the Lockheed didn't seem to respond. The Briton was aware that a helicopter tends to burst apart in a crash. He tried not to think of it as the undercarriage of the chopper smashed into the branches of treetops.

The crippled copter smashed through the thin top branches, hit a fork-shaped lower limb and came to a halt. McCarter unstrapped himself from the pilot's seat and scrambled into the cabin. The Lockheed shifted its balance among the limbs. The uninjured Italian paratrooper had helped his friend out of the harness. McCarter grabbed the wounded man under his right armpit and hooked an arm around his chest.

"Let's go!" he instructed the other paratrooper.

McCarter kicked open the sliding door and hauled the wounded man to the threshold. He grabbed a branch with his free hand and jammed a boot between a limb and tree trunk for a foothold. The other Italian trooper grabbed a branch and held on to his injured buddy as the Lockheed tipped over the edge of the limbs.

The chopper crashed upside down to the ground. The metal roof caved in and the undercarriage folded like an accordion. Glass burst from the windows and gasoline leaked from the ruptured fuel tank. The craft didn't burst into flames or explode, much to the relief of McCarter and the two carabinieri troopers, who clung to the tree twenty feet above the wrecked chopper.

"Well," McCarter remarked breathlessly, "I'd say that worked out rather well."

17

Argon Vlore helped Ahmed Kastiroti to his feet. Blood oozed from a shrapnel wound in the other man's right thigh. The ambush had not gone as well as he had hoped. The men in the trucks had proved to be better trained and better armed than Vlore had suspected. The helicopter attack had also caught the Albanian forces off guard.

Half his men were already dead or wounded and unable to fight. The Albanians had killed a number of their opponents, but the survivors had advanced while the helicopter had launched its attack. The battle was rapidly becoming a combat at close quarters. The defenders lobbed hand grenades at the Albanians' position. The explosions claimed the lives of more of Vlore's men and forced the others to stay down.

Katz, James, Inspector Krleza and a number of Italian and Yugoslavian fighters charged into the heart of the enemy position, automatic weapons blazing. Neither side would use grenades or rocket launchers at such close range due to the risk to their own people. Half a dozen Albanians were chopped down by a barrage of automatic fire when the Phoenix pair and their allies closed in.

Zog Carcani and several other Albanians returned fire. One of the Yugoslavians cried out and fell with two 7.62 mm slugs in his chest. Katz braced his Uzi across his artificial arm and sprayed the enemy with a long burst of 9 mm parabellums. Two opponents performed a grotesque death dance as their bodies jerked from the impact of the high-velocity bullets.

The pair fell lifeless to the ground, but another Albanian launched himself at Katz. The man's M-70 assault rifle had been damaged by a grenade blast, which had also sheared off two fingers from his left hand. This didn't prevent the pain-crazed and furious Albanian from grabbing the rifle by the barrel and swinging it as a club.

Katz saw the man attack as he was blasting the other two Albanians. He turned to deal with the deranged opponent as the guy swung his broken rifle. The metal stock struck the Uzi subgun from Katz's left hand. With a joyous shout, the Albanian swung his rifle again, butt stock aimed at the Israeli's skull.

The Phoenix pro ducked beneath the whirling rifle and slashed the steel hooks of his prosthesis across the attacker's right wrist. The Albanian cried out in pain as sharp metal ripped flesh and scraped bone. The rifle slipped from his grasp.

Katz jabbed his left fist to the point of his opponent's jaw. The Albanian's head snapped back. Katz immediately plunged the hooks at the end of his right arm into the man's exposed throat. Sharp steel crushed the Albanian's windpipe and ripped out the thyroid cartilage. The man staggered backward, choking to death on his own blood. Then his knees buckled and he fell to the ground.

Zog Carcani, having witnessed Katz take out the larger, younger Albanian, swung his assault rifle at the Israeli. The Phoenix veteran saw Carcani lean around a tree trunk with the M-70 blaster. Katz immediately threw himself to the ground and yanked his SiG Sauer P-226 from shoulder leather. Carcani's rifle spit a salvo of 7.62 mm slugs that hissed above the Israeli's prone form.

Katz returned fire with his P-226. His first 9 mm round struck Carcani in the left shoulder. The bullet jerked Carcani sideways and pulled him farther from cover. Katz shot him again, pumping the second parabellum slug into the center of the Albanian's chest. Carcani staggered from the impact of the second bullet and the terrible pain of his sternum bursting apart. Katz fired the SiG Sauer once more. The third round drilled into Carcani's heart and pitched his body to the ground. The Albanian's dying form performed two feeble twitches and ceased to live.

ARGON VLORE AND AHMED KASTIROTI moved away from the heart of the battle. The Albanian superspy and his wounded comrade moved deeper into the forest. Vlore hooked one of Kastiroti's arms around his neck and held his 9 mm Glock pistol in his other hand.

Kastiroti carried Vlore's Steyr SSG sniper rifle, barrel in his fist and the butt stamping the ground with each step as he used the rifle as a crutch.

"You should go on without me, Comrade Major," Kastiroti said through clenched teeth. "I will make my final prayer to Allah before He takes my soul."

"I'm getting you out of the line of fire, my friend," Vlore said, groaning under the strain. "You can make whatever prayers you like, but don't count on dying. I plan to take you back with me when we return to Albania."

"We're losing the battle, Major," Kastiroti commented. "But you are going back to fight after you get me to safety, correct?"

"It's my responsibility," Vlore answered. "I'm in command. I can't leave my men now."

"I know you do not believe in God, Major," Kastiroti stated. "But I shall pray for the mercy of Allah for your soul as well. You are a good man and I have been honored to serve under you, Major."

"I only wish it had been in different circumstances, Ahmed," Vlore said with a sigh. "This mission was wrong from the start. It was wrong for Director Progen to order it and it was wrong for us to come here."

Suddenly Major Mario Bianco appeared in front of the pair. The Italian officer had seen them heading away from the battle and had run forward to cut off their path. Bianco pointed his Beretta rifle at the two Albanians.

"Do you speak Italian?" he demanded. "How about English? I have to tell you somehow to surrender—"

Ahmed Kastiroti shoved Vlore off balance and pushed his commander to the ground. Kastiroti raised the Steyr rifle, but he didn't have a round chambered even if he could have reached the trigger before Bianco fired his Beretta. The Italian major drilled three rounds left of center in Kastiroti's chest. The Albanian lieutenant dropped the Steyr and fell beside it.

Argon Vlore returned fire with his Glock autoloader. He blasted a 9 mm round under Bianco's solar plexus. The Italian staggered and swung his Beretta toward Vlore's position. The Albanian triggered his pistol as fast as he could. The Glock snarled twice more. Bianco's head recoiled as both 9 mm slugs punched through his skull. The Italian officer was dead before he hit the ground.

"Ahmed!" Vlore rasped as he knelt beside his fallen comrade. Kastiroti's lifeless eyes stared back at him. The man's bullet-ruptured heart had stopped beating.

Vlore gently placed two fingers to Kastiroti's eyelids and pushed them shut. He'd seen a lot of men die, but most had been strangers. Vlore felt sadness and a genuine sense of loss as he lowered his head.

"I hope you find Allah, my friend," Vlore whispered.

"Freeze!" Gary Manning ordered as he pointed his Walther P-5 pistol at the back of Vlore's skull. "Try anything and I'll take your head off."

The Canadian had arrived at the scene scant seconds after Vlore had killed Major Bianco. He had found the Albanian officer kneeling next to his slain comrade. The sight was rather sad, almost touching, yet Manning was not about to let the guy walk because he could relate to the Albanian's grief at the loss of a friend.

"Drop the gun, fella," Manning warned, hoping the man understood his tone even if he did not understand English. "I'll kill you if I have to."

Vlore tossed the Glock pistol into the shadows. It landed among some bushes with a faint rustle. The Albanian slowly raised his hands and climbed to his feet. He turned to face Manning. The Canadian stood eight feet away and didn't intend to get any closer.

"You are American?" Vlore asked in rusty English. Of all his languages this was the one he had used the least.

"I'm the guy with the gun," Manning answered. He looked at Vlore's face and recalled the files the KGB had provided for Phoenix Force in Belgrade. "Pretty good plastic surgery, but I think I've seen your face before. Argon Vlore, correct?"

"Does it matter?" the Albanian said with a shrug as he stepped forward.

"Don't try it, mister," Manning warned, pointing the Walther at Vlore's face. I don't want to kill you...."

"Really?" Vlore said with a smile. "I want to kill *you*."

He suddenly bolted forward, ducking low and lashing out with both arms. It was a desperate move and Vlore would have been killed instantly if Manning had not hesitated to squeeze the trigger. The Canadian would not have been reluctant to shoot an armed opponent, but his finger didn't respond fast enough when faced with an unarmed foe.

The Walther roared a split second too late. Vlore had already moved out of the line of fire and swatted a hand under Manning's wrist to knock the pistol toward the sky. The Walther fired a 9 mm round harmlessly into the gloomy heavens.

Vlore hooked a kick to Manning's abdomen. The Canadian gasped and folded at the middle. Vlore chopped the side of a hand across Manning's wrist to strike the Walther from his grasp. He swung another karate chop at Manning's neck, but his hand struck a shoulder instead. The Canadian had turned sharply to lash out with his left fist.

Manning's knuckles crashed into Vlore's face. The Albanian's head bounced and his nostrils filled with blood. Manning drove a right uppercut to Vlore's solar plexus. The Albanian grunted, but swiftly grabbed Manning's forearms to hold down both limbs as he rammed a knee into the Canadian's groin. The knee-kick missed its mark and struck Manning's thigh.

Vlore swung a short right cross to Manning's jaw. The Albanian had a good punch and Manning's head recoiled from the blow. Yet he still lashed out with an overhead left that clipped Vlore just above the temple. Manning followed with a right uppercut under the guy's jaw.

Dazed by the punches, the Albanian stumbled backward. Manning closed in to finish him off. Vlore threw a snap kick for Manning's abdomen. The Canadian chopped his hand across Vlore's shin to stop the kick from connecting. Pain lanced the Albanian's leg, yet he hooked a left punch to Manning's face. The Phoenix pro stumbled sideways from the unexpected blow and Vlore hooked a kick to his rib cage.

Manning collided with a tree trunk. He turned and saw the flash of Vlore's right arm. The Canadian dodged the attack and Vlore's hand chopped into the tree. As a bone popped the Albanian groaned in pain. Manning hit him with a left jab to the breastbone, followed by a right cross to the jaw.

Vlore tasted blood as he staggered backward on unsteady legs. Something rolled loose in his mouth. A tooth, he realized as he spit it out. He thrust a kick for Manning's crotch.

The Canadian blocked the attack with crossed wrists and grabbed Vlore's ankle and foot. He twisted the captured leg and pushed hard to send Vlore hurtling into another tree trunk. The Albanian hit the hard walnut surface—headfirst. His skull cracked and neck vertebrae crunched. Argon Vlore embraced the tree trunk and slumped lifeless to the ground.

"There you are!" David McCarter announced as he jogged toward Manning. "We wondered what happened to you. Say, looks like you had yourself a bit of a donnybrook here."

"Yeah," Manning replied wearily. He checked on Vlore's neck for a pulse and found none. "It's over now. I'm glad you're okay. Saw your chopper go down."

"Bloody hell," the Briton snorted. "Wound up in a tree. Took us a while to get down and by the time we did the fighting was pretty much over. Our blokes won, of course. Yakov and Cal are okay. Some of the others didn't make it. Mihailo got a bullet in the forearm, but he'll be okay. Nobody seems to be able to find Bianco. Afraid he might have bought it this time."

"Sooner or later we all will," Manning stated grimly. "But it looks like this mission is all wrapped up."

"Our part of it, anyway," McCarter said cheerfully. "All that's left now is for the politicians to decide what they want to claim to be the truth. I guess we'll hear about that in a couple of days."

"The hell with it," Manning muttered. "Let's go."

18

Two days later, the government of Yugoslavia officially announced that the shooting at the American embassy had been the work of an Albanian nationalist terrorist group, which had also been responsible for the deaths of two Soviet officials and other acts of terrorism. This terrorist group had been crushed and all members of the organization were either dead or awaiting deportation to Albania.

The United States congratulated Yugoslavia on its success in handling this situation and reaffirmed the friendly relations between the two nations. The Soviet Union also announced that its investigation confirmed the reports from Belgrade, and Russia would continue both diplomatic and trade relations with Yugoslavia. Moscow even praised Yugoslavia for its sense of justice and control in a politically volatile situation.

Finally, the People's Socialist Republic of Albania announced that it would accept the Albanian nationalists expelled from Yugoslavia as a gesture of friendship toward the other nation. It officially condemned such terrorism and assured the world in general that Albania and Yugoslavia would continue to have diplomatic relations and conduct trade in the future. The Albanian press release also declared that the recent incidents in Belgrade were "shocking" and "regrettable" and hoped these dreadful events would not be repeated in the future.

The Albanian government also stated that the recently formed Security Enforcement Council had been dissolved following the untimely death of Director Haxhi Progen, who had apparently committed suicide after suffering for many months from an advanced stage of cancer.

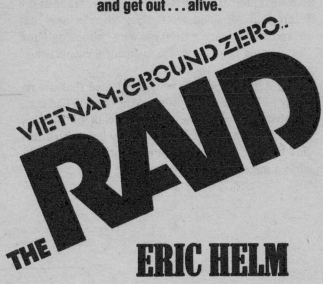

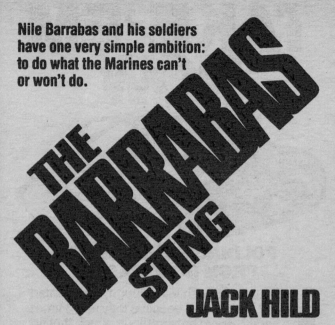

TAKE 'EM NOW

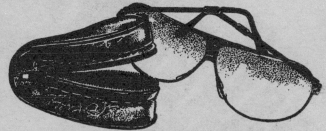

FOLDING SUNGLASSES
FROM GOLD EAGLE

Mean up your act with these tough, street-smart shades. Practical, too, because they fold 3 times into a handy, zip-up polyurethane pouch that fits neatly into your pocket. Rugged metal frame. Scratch-resistant acrylic lenses. Best of all, they can be yours for only $6.99.

MAIL YOUR ORDER TODAY.

Send your name, address, and zip code, along with a check or money order for just $6.99 + .75¢ for postage and handling (for a total of $7.74) payable to Gold Eagle Reader Service. (New York and Iowa residents please add applicable sales tax.)

Remove from pouch...

unfold once...

unfold twice...

and they're ready to wear.

Offer not available in Canada.